MAVERICK

A former U.S. marshal wrongly convicted of a bank robbery, Clayton McKinley escapes from a working party. He makes his way back to his home town, determined to expose the real perpetrators of the crime. He stumbles across an old drifter who, it seems, could be the vital witness. But it just wasn't as simple as that and, indeed, only the tenacity of Giles Wilson could give him a chance of clearing his name — and saving his hide!

L. D. TETLOW

MAVERICK

Complete and Unabridged

LINFORD
Leicester

First published in Great Britain in 1996 by
Robert Hale Limited
London

First Linford Edition
published 1998
by arrangement with
Robert Hale Limited
London

British Library CIP Data

Tetlow, L. D.
Maverick.—Large print ed.—
Linford western library
1. Western stories
2. Large type books
I. Title
823.9'14 [F]

ISBN 0–7089–5201–1

Published by
F. A. Thorpe (Publishing) Ltd.
Anstey, Leicestershire

Set by Words & Graphics Ltd.
Anstey, Leicestershire
Printed and bound in Great Britain by
T. J. International Ltd., Padstow, Cornwall

This book is printed on acid-free paper

1

AS far as Clay McKinley was concerned, society owed him a debt, a debt it had incurred when Judge James Madison had passed sentence upon him of fifteen years' hard labour for a crime he had not committed — the armed robbery of a bank, during the course of which a bank clerk had been killed. He had often wondered if Judge Madison would have passed such a severe sentence had not he, Clay McKinley, been entrusted with the office of Federal Marshal of the United States, a position of which he had been more than proud and had strived hard to achieve.

Now, something over three years and two months later — according to his calculations — Clay McKinley stared down upon the town of Lewis from the relative safety of the high ridge which swept around its southern end, noting that even in that comparatively short time the changes had transformed the once sleepy town almost beyond recognition.

Now there were large corrals and pens to the south and east and a railroad passed east to west with a spur line down to the corrals and a station now occupied the site of what had once been a disused church. A new church had now appeared in the centre of the town. He had been at the forefront of efforts to bring the railroad to Lewis but had not had time to see the fruits of his efforts.

Three years?

It had taken that long for the opportunity to escape to arise. There had been brief moments when he had seriously considered breaking out or even murdering a guard whilst on a work detail, but he had always shied away from actual murder. On other occasions serious discussion had taken place between himself and other prisoners and escapes had been planned, but once again something had always warned him that the time was not ripe. More than once his instincts had proved right when others with whom he might have escaped had been gunned down with little attempt made to recapture them.

Prior to his own imprisonment, Clay McKinley had had no sympathy at all for the men he helped to incarcerate in that same prison. His attitude had always been that if a man — or woman — broke the law, then they must accept whatever punishment was meted out to them. The concept of innocent men being subjected to the degrading horrors of life in the State Penitentiary had never really crossed his mind, his belief in the justice and fairness of the legal system being such that he had refused to accept that innocent men or women could ever be convicted. His own conviction and the three years he had been in prison had changed all that.

Perhaps he had had it worse than a great many other men since he was suddenly forced to rub shoulders with men he had brought to justice and the guards appeared to treat him worse than other prisoners simply because he had been a US Marshal. Whatever the reason, Clay McKinley knew that he had been very lucky to have survived three years, just as he knew that the chances of him seeing out the fifteen years of his sentence were almost nil. Sheer determination, the fact that he was a big, powerful man and well able to hold his own in any fight had been the things that had seen him through.

* * *

Escape, when the first real opportunity had arisen, had happened quite unexpectedly and he wondered if anyone guessed or sensed that he was alive.

He and nine other prisoners, along with three armed guards, had been detailed to repair the trail which had

4

been washed away during a storm. They had repaired the road and were heading back when another storm struck with a ferocity Clay had never witnessed before. They had been travelling in the prison wagon along the road about seven or eight miles from the prison, high above a swollen river, when the ground had suddenly given way and all had been plunged into the swollen, muddy waters.

How he had survived he had no idea, but he gave brief thanks to Heaven and managed to struggle from the caged prison wagon. The nine other prisoners were plainly dead, one guard had somehow had his head almost severed, a second lay sprawled face down in the water, his legs trapped between two rocks and he caught sight of the body of the third guard being swirled downstream. A quick examination of the prison wagon showed that the back bars had been wrenched away and one body was already being drawn through the opening by the current. He had been quite satisfied that searchers would have no reason to believe that anyone had survived, especially when the body of the guard was discovered further downstream.

Clay did look around for one of the rifles carried by the guards, but none were to be found and he had no intention of diving into the muddy waters in an attempt to find one. Of the two horses pulling the wagon, one was dead and the other, although still alive, so badly injured as to be no use at all. He had walked away from the scene taking care not to leave any obvious signs.

★ ★ ★

Lewis held the key to proving his innocence. In that town he knew that there were some people who knew a whole lot more than they had ever testified to. In fact he had been convinced at the time and was even more convinced now that the real culprits were otherwise respectable residents of the town.

Shortly after his conviction Clay had heard that certain well-known figures had suddenly come into sufficient funds to be able to pay off various debts. Looking down on the town now he wondered how much of that money had also influenced the railroad company in taking their line through Lewis.

Clay was, along with two unknown accomplices, supposed to have escaped with a little over $500,000, a sum even Clay had difficulty in appreciating just how much that really was. The clincher had been when $10,000 had been discovered in his house and which had been easily identifiable being new notes with the numbers in sequence. It had all been a little too convenient but even he had had to admit that he would have readily believed the evidence.

The only thing he had ever been thankful for was that he had never married. Not that he had not had the opportunity, he just never seemed to have the time.

★ ★ ★

Since escaping, there had only been one thought on Clay's mind, to seek out those actually guilty of the robbery and thus prove his own innocence, but now, so close to his target and with time to reflect, it suddenly dawned on him that if he had been presumed dead after the accident he was, in practically every respect, a free man. Free to go where he chose and free to take on a new identity. The need to prove his innocence had largely been taken away from him.

Clay mulled the problem over in his mind since at that moment he had very little else to do. To venture into the town in broad daylight would bring instant recognition and almost certain arrest by the town sheriff, a hard but fair man by the name of Giles Wilson — at least it had been Giles who had been sheriff when he lived in the town. As a US Marshal, Clay had had little do with the running of the town, it was simply his home base. Clay knew, despite the friendship that had been between them and Giles's stated belief that Clay was innocent, that Giles would have no hesitation in arresting him and handing him over to the authorities. He would probably have done the same.

However, apart from his deep-rooted desire to prove his innocence, Clay had two more immediate and probably more pressing problems, without which any attempts to find proof would be useless — a horse and a hand gun at the very least, with a rifle thrown in if he could get one.

He had made the 200-mile journey from the prison to Lewis on foot, avoiding towns and the occasional traveller and grubbing his food the best he could off the land. Once he did come across a farm which, although obviously inhabited, was completely empty with some very tempting, freshly baked food. He had wrapped some up in a cloth and taken it with him and he had searched the house for a gun and money, not finding a gun except for an ancient muzzle-loading rifle with no powder or shot and exactly three dollars and fourteen cents in cash. The money was still intact in his pocket.

More than once he had even considered waylaying one of the infrequent travellers and stealing his clothes, horse and gun and possibly even killing the man to protect himself. It had in actual fact been the thought that he would more than likely have to kill such a traveller which had prevented him.

Clothes! That was another thing Clay needed. His prison uniform which, although plain and unmarked, was obviously what it was, a uniform and as such hardly likely to fool anyone, especially any lawman he might come across.

Clay settled down in the shade

of the thick bushes overlooking the plain, waiting for nightfall when he would probably venture into town and possibly steal what he needed since he knew where everything was and even the weak points of various stores. He glanced up at the sun, which seemed to indicate some time in mid-afternoon, stroked his heavily bearded face and pulled the tattered hat he had found in a derelict building over his eyes and closed them.

A smile suddenly crossed his weathered features as it dawned on him that he must look very different now. Three years previously he had been clean-shaven, fair-haired and smooth-skinned. Now he was bearded, dirty-haired and with weathered skin and gnarled features. He smiled again as he thought that he would have difficulty in recognizing even himself from that distance of time. However, he was still not prepared to take the chance of being recognised, at least not yet. When he was ready he would reveal himself.

★ ★ ★

He did not sleep, although to anyone passing by it would have appeared so. Most of the time was spent studying the comings and goings of Lewis through half-closed eyes, occasionally opening them wider to study something of interest.

There did not appear to be very much activity in or around the corrals and pens except that there was one small paddock close to a building he did not recognize which contained about six horses and what appeared to be at least two saddles straddling the fence. As to which day it was, he honestly did not have the faintest idea. The only thing he was reasonably certain of was that it was not Sunday since there had been no evidence of activity in and around the church and all other activity was in keeping with a normal day, but that day could be any one of six as far as Clay was concerned.

Not that what day it was was in

any way of the slightest importance, it was simply a matter of curiosity. Three years in prison had destroyed all sense of time at least in the sense of knowing which day it was and even his supposed efforts at recording the days by carving notches on pieces of wood seemed meaningless other than convincing him that it was now three years, two months and three days since his imprisonment, although now he was even uncertain as to which month it was. He thought it was July but he could not be too certain, but again it did not matter; it was more a case of attempting to rationalize and establish his identity once again.

Rationalization of his surroundings, of time and of purpose now assumed a role far greater than it had been in prison where all such things were largely beaten out of prisoners. It was important to him to place himself in the present day order of things and thereby, he believed, regain his lost years and identity.

He had been lying and watching for about an hour when sounds behind him made him hide, making the mistake of choosing a thorn bush and having to grimace and grit his teeth as the big thorns dug into his flesh. However, the thorns did have the effect of forcing him to keep very still and very quiet as two figures slowly rode out from behind him and on to the ridge, turning to follow the edge and seeming to look directly at him.

Clay bit his lip and gritted his teeth as he recognized the one figure as that of Giles Wilson who now wore the badge of office of a marshal. The other figure he thought was that of a young deputy at the time of his trial, who now was plainly town sheriff.

Clay was almost convinced that the pair had seen him, but he sighed with relief and then cursed silently as thorns dug deeper into his flesh, as the two men rode by, talking and laughing. Clay allowed them about ten minutes before he eased himself painfully from the embrace of the thorn bush.

At least now he knew who he was dealing with should the necessity arise, which he sincerely hoped would not. The last thing he wanted was a confrontation with the man who, for a good many years, had been one of his closest friends.

About half an hour later he saw the two lawmen riding across the plain towards Lewis and at the same time there appeared to be a lot more activity in the town. There was nothing unusual in this, it was normal for most people to avoid the heat of the afternoon indoors and resume activity in the cool of the evening.

All this time Clay had been thinking, thinking about whom he could trust and could not trust and, despite their earlier friendship, he decided that Giles Wilson would definitely fall into the latter category — he was a very good and conscientious lawman. In fact, he came to the conclusion that there was probably only one man whom he could trust; Mick Hartford, owner of what had, three years previously, been the only general store in Lewis.

Mick Hartford had been the only man who had maintained a belief in Clay's innocence, even when presented with the evidence of the stolen money. True, others had, in the early days, also proclaimed their belief in Clay's innocence, but in almost every case the outward signs of support had evaporated as time wore on and at the trial there had been but one lone voice in support, that of Mick Hartford.

Clay's need for a gun, a horse and some fresh clothes was paramount and he decided that Mick was the only man he could approach. Once again he settled down and waited. He would venture into Lewis after dark.

★ ★ ★

The lights from oil lamps glowed weakly as Clay climbed down the ridge, taking care to avoid the trail since he did not want to chance meeting anyone. He thought that he knew the terrain pretty well since he had scaled the sides of the ridge many times in the past, but it seemed rougher and had a lot more holes than he remembered, although he put this down to the fact that it was now almost pitch black and difficult to see more than a step in front of himself. After what seemed like hours later, he was on the level and making steadier progress.

Whilst he had been descending the ridge, the lights of Lewis had been plain to see, but down on the flat, they suddenly disappeared and only when he came to a small mound could he see any lights at all and once discovered that he was heading in the wrong direction. He knew that from the base of the ridge to the town was two miles, but in the dark that two miles seemed more like ten. Eventually however, he found himself following the line of a corral fence and the dim glow of oil lamps gradually became brighter and clearer.

He remembered the paddock in which he had seen the horses and what appeared to be saddles on the fence and made this his first priority. What had seemed plain and obvious from the vantage of the ridge now proved rather more difficult but eventually he found the paddock still with its horses and, sure enough, what he had thought were saddles were just that. At least that solved one of his problems.

Three years earlier, finding his way to Mick Hartford's store without being seen would have been easy, but as he made his way around the rear of various buildings he suddenly found himself faced with walls, fences and other buildings that had not been there before and he was forced to make even greater detours.

Time and the changing face of Lewis made him lose his sense of direction slightly and when he peered around the edge of a building, he discovered that he was no more than a couple of hundred yards along the main street from the point he had started and almost directly opposite the sheriff's office.

In the office, brightly lit by the same three oil lamps which been there in his day, he could see the young man who now appeared to have assumed the role of town sheriff. Although he had known the man as a deputy, he could not remember his name, but he did not try too hard, he had more important matters to attend.

A glance along the street showed that Mick Hartford's general store was still there but, whereas at one time it had been the largest building in town, it was now almost dwarfed by what appeared to be a hotel alongside. Obviously the coming of the railroad had also brought other demands upon the town of Lewis. He made his way back along the alley and continued his tortuous detour.

The next time he made his way

down an alleyway, he found himself alongside the new hotel and going by the sound of music and chatter of voices inside, it obviously offered rather more than a normal hotel. He eventually discovered that it was also a gambling hall, something which would have been rigorously opposed by the ladies of the town a few years earlier.

Mick Hartford's store was now on his right and, after checking that this was so, Clay made his way back down the alley and found a wooden gate which opened easily and he entered the small yard and waited, fully expecting the large dog which Mick had always kept to come bounding at him, but he knew from experience that if he did not move the dog would not attack. However, there was no dog and no sound of one inside. Quietly he stepped forward and knocked on the back door of what had been Mick's living quarters.

"Lookin' for somethin', mister?" The voice was quiet but firm and the barrel of the rifle now dug firmly in Clay's back was even firmer.

"I'm lookin' for Mick Hartford," replied Clay, raising his hands.

"You found him," rasped the voice, digging the barrel in harder. "Normal folk use the shop door. What makes you so different?"

"What happened to Bruce?" asked Clay, keeping very still.

"Bruce?" queried Mick. "What the hell do you know about Bruce?"

"I know me an' him was great friends once."

"Bruce is dead," rasped Mick, "been dead almost two years, shot by someone breakin' in. Now answer the question, who are you an' what do you want?"

"Clay McKinley!" replied Clay. "I need your help."

"Clay McKinley!" grated Mick. "Clay's dead, everyone knows that." The rifle bit deeper and Clay winced.

"Then you'd better believe in ghosts," said Clay. "Maybe if we go inside I can convince you."

"Maybe we'd be better goin' to see the sheriff," said Mick. "I knew Clay McKinley pretty damned good an' you may be about the same height, but you sure ain't his build an' you don't sound like him."

"Three years in prison ain't a whole lot of good to a man's muscles," replied Clay. "As for my voice, I don't know."

"Open the door," ordered Mick, prodding the gun into Clay's back. "If you're Clay, I'll know. If you ain't, make one move an' you're a dead man."

"I've grown a beard," said Clay as he opened the door and stepped into the lighted room.

Mick Hartford followed and stared hard at the man now facing him. "Hell, even with the beard an' takin' into account how weather-beaten an' dirty you are, you sure could pass for Clay McKinley."

"That's 'cos I am," smiled Clay. "How else would I know about your dog, Bruce?"

Mick's hold on the rifle did not waver as he studied the features again. "Clay had a scar on his left arm," he said eventually. "Let's see if you have one."

Clay smiled and pulled up the sleeve of his tattered jacket to reveal a half-moon shaped scar. "The only time Bruce ever bit me," he grinned. "Now do you believe who I am? One thing's for certain, I sure ain't dead, leastways if I am, I ain't noticed no difference an' I guess I'd be just about the first to know."

The rifle dropped to the floor and Mick suddenly embraced his old friend. Eventually he pulled back and looked Clay up and down. "Clay McKinley, as I live an' breathe it is you. I gotta admit though I'd've passed you by in the street not knowin' who the hell you were. You're supposed to be dead. We heard some weeks ago that you an' some others had been drowned when a landslide washed you into a river."

"That's what happened sure enough,"

grinned Clay. "Only thing was I didn't drown, as you can see. All the others died, includin' the guards. I guess they just assumed I'd been washed away in the river."

"Somethin' like that from what I hear," said Mick, dragging out a chair and forcing Clay to sit down. "They found the body of one guard more'n ten miles downstream. I did hear they never found your body . . . " He grinned sheepishly. "But I guess that's obvious. Apparently they searched the area just in case you were still alive but they found no evidence so they assumed your body had been washed away."

"Which makes me a free man I guess," smiled Clay. "If I'm officially dead they can't arrest me for breakin' out."

Mick laughed. "I wouldn't hold too much store by that if I was you. Both Giles an' Joe Turner wouldn't turn a hair at runnin' you in an' handin' you over, dead or not."

"I saw Giles an' the new sheriff up on the ridge," said Clay. "I see Giles is now a marshal."

"An' has been since just after you was sent to prison," replied Mick as he reached into a cupboard and took out two glasses and a bottle of the finest Scotch whisky. "Hugh Styles took over as sheriff for about twelve months but then he suddenly died, heart attack or somethin', that's when young Joe Turner took over. He may be young but he's good an' ain't scared of nothin' an' nobody." He poured out two large measures of whisky and handed one to Clay who looked at it appreciatively for a while. "Go on, drink it," grinned Mick. "I reckon that's just about the first decent drink you've seen for more'n three years."

Clay smiled and nodded and raised the glass to his lips, sipping and savouring. He ventured a larger sip and suddenly lurched forward spluttering and coughing. "Christ!" he oathed. "Just shows I ain't used to it." He placed the glass on the table and fingered it almost lovingly. "I'll take the first one gentle like." He glanced up at Mick. "Ain't you goin' to ask just what the hell I'm doin' here?"

Mick smiled, drained his glass and poured out another measure. "I figure you'll tell me when you're ready. Right now though I'd say what you needed most was a hot bath an' a comfortable bed. We can talk about it in the mornin'."

Clay nodded. "I guess I must smell somethin' pretty disgustin'," he grinned. "We had a sort of bath once a month in prison, but I ain't had one for three months now. I hate to put on an old friend, but have you got some decent clothes I can change into?"

"Got a whole shopful!" grinned Mick. "First though, I'll see to your bath . . . "

2

MICK HARTFORD had insisted that Clay should have a good night's sleep before discussing anything and since the next day was Sunday the store did not open at all. Very few traders opened on a Sunday in Lewis, they considered it a day of rest and churchgoing. Neither of them thought it would be a good idea for Clay to attend church, although he had always been a regular church-goer and always taken part in the infrequent services in prison.

Clay had to confess that he had spent a rather sleepless night but that it was not due in any part to matters which might be on his mind, but to the simple fact that it had been so long since he had slept in a comfortable bed that he had forgotten how.

Neither Clay nor Mick were men

who normally partook of breakfast; that meal as far as they were concerned usually consisted of two cheroots and a large mug of coffee followed by much retching, swearing and coughing. Although he had long got out of the habit, it did not take Clay many minutes to fall into the routine once again.

Mick left his friend to lounge in an easy chair whilst he went off to church, returning an hour later. There had been a Mrs Hartford a few years earlier, but she had died in childbirth, as had the child and Mick had never really recovered from the experience and had never shown any interest in women as marriage partners since that time.

New clothes had been provided, including a much needed pair of boots, new underwear and socks and, after looking at his bearded reflection with a much jaundiced eye for a few moments, Clay opted to retain the beard and ask Mick his opinion.

Until that point, clothes had been

something that simply had to be worn; he had never appreciated the good, clean feel of new underwear and a new shirt. Now he looked at himself in a long mirror, turned this way and that, much as he had seen women do when wearing a new dress, felt a complete fool and was very glad there was nobody to see his antics, but he felt more human again.

"The beard," he said to Mick when the latter returned from church. "Shave it off or keep it?"

"You'd be a bloody fool to shave it off just yet," advised Mick. "There's too many folk in town who'd recognize you an' I have this feelin' that there's more'n one person who was mighty glad to hear that you were killed."

"Yeh," muttered Clay. "That's another thing I have to talk to you about. I didn't do that robbery, you know that . . . " Mick nodded his head. "An' as far as I can see it sure wasn't done by no regular outlaws or outsiders. I said at the time an' I still say that it was done by otherwise solid, upright citizens of Lewis."

Mick gave Clay a cheroot and eased himself into the easy chair opposite, drew on the cheroot and blew a smoke ring into the air before replying. "All I can say is that one or two folk suddenly seemed to have a whole lot more money than they ever had before. Just after you were sent away, the railroad company suddenly agreed to come this way. I ain't sayin' that a few palms were greased or anythin', but up to that point they had always insisted it was too far out of their way to be worthwhile. I think that a certain official saw the error of his ways after he found about ten thousand dollars in his bags. I know that 'cos he got drunk and blabbed his mouth off to Maisie Stobbs an' she told me. Anyhow, she must have told someone else 'cos just after the go-ahead for the track to come through here had been given, this certain railroad official was accidentally thrown from a horse an' broke his neck an' died. Now that could've been an accident, but it sure was a convenient one."

"Who was he ridin' with at the time?" asked Clay.

"From what I hear, Peter Turnbull, the president of the bank as was, an' Hans Gerhart. You must remember Hans, he was a strugglin' rancher then but he suddenly found the money to buy out Grant Thompson an' now he's just about the biggest rancher in these parts."

"What happened to Turnbull?" asked Clay. "You said 'as was'."

"Retired about a month after the railroad came, died about two months ago. Doc says it was a heart attack but the amount he ate and drank I'd say it was over-indulgence."

"Anyone else who suddenly came into money?" asked Clay.

"Real money?" mused Mick. "Jim Proud an' Tom Walker. Jim Proud went back East somewhere an' I did hear he bought himself some sort of farm or estate or somethin'. Tom Walker is still right here, in fact he's now my new next-door-neighbour. He built the hotel. There were one or two small-time folk who seemed to have money to throw away all of a sudden, but not that much. I'd say they were paid to keep quiet."

"I suppose it could all just be coincidence," said Clay, "but I can't really believe that. I had the feelin' that Turnbull had been in difficulty with the bank for some time. I think he'd been helping himself to deposits and was in danger of bein' found out. If he wasn't directly involved, that robbery sure solved a lot of his problems. It's a pity he's dead, now we'll never know for sure. That leaves Gerhart an' Walker."

Mick sighed and shook his head. "Personally I don't think you're goin' to be able to prove a thing. I don't know if you know it or not, but Giles Wilson tried his damnedest to prove you were innocent an' he made himself a few enemies an' even now he still ain't the most popular man in town. It's only the fact that he was made marshal an' as such has no direct influence here that he's more or less accepted."

"Maybe I should talk to him first an' find out what he knows," mused Clay. "Only thing is, I know he's a good lawman an' as such he'll be bound to arrest me an' send me back to prison."

Once again Mick shrugged, poured himself another drink and looked approvingly for a few moments, turning the glass round in his hand and finally drank the contents in one gulp.

"You're dead, remember, an' that's official. There ain't nothin' you can do to change what's happened. Take my advice, just take advantage of the situation an' get the hell well away from here an' start a new life. Change your name, find yourself a good woman an' settle down."

Clay laughed. "Yeh, I've got to admit

that there's many still in prison who'd give their eye teeth to be declared dead. Maybe I'm just being plain awkward about it all, but I've thought of nothin' else for three years an' the thought of givin' up on all that now just don't sit easy with me. I have to know the truth."

"I reckon you an' me both know the truth, Clay," smiled Mick. "It ain't knowin' the truth you want, it's revenge an' as I see it, the law is all on their side an' stacked up against you. Do yourself a favour, keep on travellin' until you're out of this state at least."

Clay laughed. "Hell, Mick, I know you're right but . . . I dunno . . . it needs some thinkin' about. I can't just give up on three years of dreamin' an' plannin' just like that. Hell, there'd be no problem if I hadn't been declared dead. I'd be on the run maybe even with Giles sent to hunt me down but at least I'd be able to put the fear of God into a few folk before I got caught. Anyhow, even if I was to listen to what you say, you saw what state I was in when I got here. Worn-out clothes, no money, no gun an' no horse so where the hell do I go, what do I do an' most of all how do I get any decent woman to take an interest in me?"

Mick smiled. "OK, no woman," he said. "It ain't bothered me none since Mary died. New clothes . . . " He nodded at Clay's legs. "I guess I can find some more. Money? Maybe some of that too. Not much, maybe fifty dollars but it'll help you on your way. It could be that I can root out a gun an' some bullets. Part of my business is takin' pledges on goods when folk is hard up — which seems quite often these days — an' it's usually guns they bring in. Mind you, I must admit that these days there just ain't no need for anyone to carry a gun. We ain't had no violence since the day the bank was robbed. The only folk you'll see in Lewis with guns are the marshal, the sheriff an' any strangers what pass through. Joe Turner allus makes it plain to strangers that if they want to stop in town they leave their guns somewhere safe."

"Sounds too good to be true," grinned Clay.

"Maybe so," nodded Mick, "but that's the way things are. I've got me several guns what are well past their redeem date, so rightly I can sell 'em or do as I please with 'em. What's your preference? I seem to remember you had a Navy Colt."

"Best gun there ever was," said Clay. "You got one?"

"Think so," nodded Mick. "That just leaves you needin' a horse."

"An' a saddle," Clay pointed out.

Mick thought for a moment and then nodded. "I got me one of them too," he smiled. "Pledged by old Isaac Lawton, you remember him, lived by himself down by the river. Well, he's been dead these past six months so he won't be needin' it. Can't help you with the horse though."

Clay smiled. "I saw some in a pen

down by the corrals, two saddles as well. I was goin' to help myself."

Mick smiled. "Unless you want to get yourself noticed, I sure wouldn't do that. Besides, them are old saddles only used by a few young bucks who fancy themselves as horse-breakers. Them horses technically don't belong to nobody I guess. They're all mavericks rounded up by the bucks, so I guess if anyone has a claim to them it's them."

"Bucks?" queried Clay.

Mick smiled and nodded understandingly. "Yeh, bucks," he grinned. "All the ranches employ either Mexicans, blacks or bucks. I'd say there ain't more 'n half-a dozen white hands in the whole territory."

"Times have changed!" smiled Clay. "Time was when nobody would employ Indians an' they didn't seem too keen either."

"No more huntin' an' havin' to live on reservations has changed all that," nodded Mick. "They do sell the horses after they've broken 'em," Mick continued. "If you like I'll go have a word with 'em . . . " He thought for a moment and smiled. "One of 'em owes me, I've got a lot of his goods pledged. Maybe I can do a deal."

"Ain't that the same as you havin' to buy?" asked Clay.

Mick shrugged. "Guess so, but at least it ain't cash out of my pocket."

Clay smiled and thought for a few moments. "If they're all mavericks, nobody'd be too surprised if they was to break out, would they?"

Mick grinned knowingly. "It happens sometimes. Sometimes too some young tearaway with nothin' better to do opens the pen an' lets 'em out."

Clay laughed. "I guess you could hardly call me a young tearaway, but who would know? All I need to know is which horses are broken an' which ain't. I sure ain't got the time to start breakin' horses now."

"Leave it to me," smiled Mick. "I'll take me a walk down there this afternoon. That's when they do most of their breakin'."

"In the meantime what do I do?" asked Clay.

"You just sit tight right here," instructed Mick. "If anyone comes you just pretend the place is empty."

★ ★ ★

Mick returned at about four o'clock with the news that there were two horses broken and ready, a chestnut and a black and white. The chestnut could be identified by a white blaze between its eyes.

"The piebald would be too easy to identify," said Mick. "Besides, I reckon she's a mite too small for you."

The saddle and the Navy Colt were found and handed to Clay who immediately set about cleaning the gun, complaining that it did not appear to have had an oily rag anywhere near it for years. However, after three or four hours of patient rubbing and polishing, he seemed satisfied. The saddle too needed some attention in the form of saddle soap and dubbin but that too looked fairly reasonable when he had finished.

"I guess I'm just about ready," grinned Clay as he practised drawing the gun. "I'll be on my way now, there don't seem much point in hangin' round, it might only get you into trouble."

Mick, true to his word, counted out fifty dollars in five dollar bills and handed them to Clay. "What's your next move? I hope you've decided to forget all about revenge an' take the chance to start over again."

"I'm still thinkin' about it," said Clay.

That was true, in fact he had been thinking of little else all day. What he did not tell his friend was that the conclusion he had arrived at was not one which would please him.

However, Clay had suddenly realized that three years in prison had done nothing to improve his draw with a hand gun and if he was to take on the powerful men of Lewis, or more probably their hired guns, he knew that he had to show them that his old skills had not deserted him. In addition, although he had not actually fired the gun, he sensed that had he done so his aim would have been well wide of target. He had the feeling that a rifle would not be that much better.

The conclusion he had come to terms with, for the moment at least, he would have to hide up somewhere in the hills, well away from prying eyes and sharp ears and hone up on his shooting skills. It would also give him more time to think and it was just possible that he might eventually come to agree with Mick and take the opportunity to start afresh. In the meantime it was important that he left town before anyone knew he was there and started asking awkward questions.

Mick did not really approve of Clay's plan to steal one of the horses, but he had to confess that he could not recommend any practical alternative. It was agreed that the saddle and some harness be left at the far end of the alley which divided Mick's store from the hotel — Mick giving Clay precise instructions how to get round the back without having to cross any other property. He also insisted that Clay take a good supply of dried meat, beans, salt and flour to help him on his way, as well as a billy-can and cooking utensils. He also gave him about 200 rounds of ammunition for the Colt.

There was nothing much that Clay could do, it was decided that the safest time to take the horse would be around midnight and, since that meant Clay would have to ride at night, he spent most of the remaining time asleep.

★ ★ ★

Both men had assumed that midnight would be the quietest part of the day, especially because it was Sunday and a working day the next day and people would tend to be abed that little bit earlier. In the event, it appeared that almost the entire population of Lewis had decided to make that particular Sunday an exception.

In his attempts to avoid being seen, Clay made his way along the rear of the properties only to find two couples locked together in passionate embrace. The woman in the second instance saw him and he heard her say to her panting partner that she had thought he was her husband.

At another point he had to hide in a deep shadow as Joe Turner, the town sheriff, suddenly appeared and for a moment it seemed that he had been seen but the sheriff suddenly turned across the street.

The biggest problem came when he was within sight of the corrals where, much to his dismay, he discovered a group of about eight young Indian bucks laughing and chanting as a bottle was passed around. Although all appeared to be very drunk, Clay knew from experience that a drunken buck was the most difficult kind. He was not too surprised at seeing them; Indians had always been barred from the saloons and bars and it appeared that this was still the case. He could do nothing but settle down under a solitary tree to wait and pretend that he too was sleeping off drunkenness should anyone appear which, to his relief, they did not.

It was certainly well past two in the morning before the last of the bucks disappeared and the town final]y seemed to close for the night. However, Clay knew the routine and, hiding himself, waited for the regular patrol around the town by the sheriff or, more likely, one of his deputies. His caution was well founded.

Two men appeared, both wearing badges of office and both carrying rifles. They stopped at the end of a boardwalk overlooking the paddock containing the horses and talked for a few moments. Clay had hidden himself in an old privy and he could see all that was happening through the broken boards. One of the deputies — that was what they appeared to be, headed straight for him and for a very brief moment Clay thought that the man was going to make use of the shack for the purpose it had been built, but he hardly gave it a glance as he passed by. Clay decided to give the men another ten minutes before leaving his hiding place.

★ ★ ★

The big chestnut was easy to identify, being the largest and the only one with a white blaze on its head. They seemed a little nervous as he approached but he was well used to semi-wild animals such as these and knew how to soothe them.

The first thing he did was to pass a rope around the neck of the chestnut and lead it out of the paddock. He lashed it firmly to a post and then returned to the paddock to urge the remaining horses out in order to make it appear someone had deliberately opened the paddock and hide the fact that he had taken the chestnut.

He would have been willing to take bets that the horses would be only too ready to make a run for freedom, but in fact they appeared almost reluctant to leave. In the event he gave up trying and decided simply to leave the gate open and hope that they would find their own way out.

Following Mick's instructions, he led the horse back to the store where he found the saddle and a couple of saddle-bags. He smiled, Mick had done him proud as usual and he felt as though he might be betraying a trust if he did come back to find out who had carried out the robbery.

Although it appeared to be broken, the horse was plainly unused to having a saddle thrown across its back and shied several times making it impossible for

Clay to throw the saddle over. He was just about to go and ask Mick Hartford to help him when he heard voices at the end of the alley. He glanced along and saw three men framed in the weak light.

One was plainly his friend, Mick Hartford, and it appeared that Mick was doing his best to prevent the other two from coming down the alley and also keeping their backs towards him. Clay looked up at the big horse and whispered, "One more time, you big lump of meat. Now I ain't goin' to hurt you, but if them men see me they just might want to hurt me an' I'm sure neither of us want that, do we?" To his surprise the horse pushed her nuzzle against him in an almost friendly gesture. "Now you keep quiet," Clay whispered again. To his amazement this time the horse kept perfectly still and allowed herself to be saddled.

When he had finished and filled the saddle-bags, Clay gave another look up the alley just in time to see the two men more or less push past Mick, all three laughing, Mick seemingly louder than the other two in what Clay could only take to be an attempt to warn him. Clay mounted and very slowly eased the horse forward away from the alley. He held his breath and hoped that the deputies did not hear the sound of the horse's hooves.

He did not look back, it seemed to make some sort of perverted logic to him that if he could not see the deputies, they could not see him. Whatever the reason, there was no call from behind and no warning shot. Still holding his breath, he kept going but his hand was on the Colt just in case . . .

3

CLAY had been giving serious thought as to where would be the best and safest place for him to hide out and had eventually come to the conclusion that some old silver workings about ten miles out of Lewis would probably be the most suitable. With his knowledge of the territory he had no difficulty in finding his way even in the dark. In actual fact dawn was breaking as he descended into the old, rough workings.

Things were almost exactly as he remembered them, a couple of derelict huts, the remains of a large washing plant with water still flowing through it and a general landscape that reminded him of drawings of what the surface of the moon was supposed to be like. A hut situated at the base of the washing plant seemed to offer the best protection from the elements, which he knew could be very cold at certain times of the year.

He felt that he would be reasonably safe since the old workings were well away from any trail and unless someone knew they were there, casual travellers would pass without knowing of the existence of the place.

A brief but fairly thorough check of the area seemed to show that he was the first to set foot there for some considerable time. There were other residents in the form of rats which scuttled away as he approached, a large owl perched high in the rafters of the old washing plant looking very fat and well fed, at least two rattlesnakes which hissed and rattled threateningly when they saw him but otherwise made no move and countless lizards, mainly small ones but there were a couple of sizeable fat-tailed specimens. Some unidentified birds took flight and several ticks lost little time in attaching themselves to his legs.

Ticks were always a problem but were normally painless unless any attempt was made to remove them, in which case their jaws and pincers were always left behind. There was only one effective way of dealing with ticks and that was to burn them off with a cheroot otherwise it was best to leave them to drop off of their own accord once they had gorged themselves with blood. He opted to leave them alone for the time-being.

Water presented no problem, the water still running through the washing plant seemed clean and wholesome and his horse, which he had decided to call Kate seemed to appreciate both the water and the grass which grew along the water course.

Clay had always called his horses Kate, quite why was lost in the mists of time, but it had been a name he had taken to when he was a boy. He had even insisted on calling a stallion he once had by that name, at least the horse did not seem to mind.

Having been awake all night, Clay decided that a few hours sleep was his first priority and after giving the hut a cursory clean out, he spread the blanket which Mick Hartford had also included and was soon asleep.

★ ★ ★

The sun was well past its height when he finally came to and since his mouth felt very dry and tasted as though one of the rats had deposited something in it, he gathered some wood and soon had his billy-can of coffee heating up. Although he had food, three years privation and near starvation had somehow dramatically reduced his desire for food.

The first thing he did when the coffee was ready was to strip off completely and set to work with the glowing end of a stick from the fire and burn off the countless ticks which had attached themselves whilst he had been asleep for a sudden and unexpected meal.

He knew the operation was largely a waste of time, he would be repeating the operation once again the following morning. In the time he had been in prison he had learned to ignore them, but it did give him a sort of perverse satisfaction to burn the offending insects off.

Once he was dressed and had his fill of coffee, he decided to take a proper look around, venturing into some of the many mine openings although not going too far in since he could not be certain as to how safe they were. All he was doing was establishing what was where should the need ever arise, although he did discover a pick and shovel in seemingly good condition in one mine and a rusting oil lamp complete with a container of what looked and smelled like lamp oil in another. The wick of the lamp seemed almost new and he tested the contents of the container in the lamp, grunting with satisfaction as the flame gave off a good, even glow.

Apart from these items, his search of the site produced nothing of note. Next he climbed the side of the workings and surveyed the surrounding countryside, although he was well aware of what it used to look like but judging by the rate change had taken place in Lewis, he was prepared for anything. As it was, everything looked exactly as he remembered it.

In the distance it was just possible to make out a herd of cows alongside the river, the river which eventually flowed past Lewis, but other than the cows, there was little sign of any human activity. This was what he had expected and, for the moment, what he wanted.

He was just about to descend into the workings when a rabbit suddenly appeared and stopped for a moment as it eyed Clay, quite plainly uncertain as to what this new creature was. Clay smiled and slowly drew his gun, took a steady aim at the still curious rabbit and squeezed the trigger.

He did not actually see which way the rabbit went, but he did see the dust fly up about three feet to the left of where the animal had been as the bullet buried itself. He had never been so disgusted with himself: an easy, sitting target which should have presented no problems even to a child, had been missed by a margin that he would have thought impossible. He shook his head and examined the Colt in disbelief as if hoping to be able to lay the blame on the gun and not his own inability. Since there did not appear to be anything wrong with the gun he was forced into the opinion that three years' inactivity with a firearm had taken a worse toll than he could have imagined.

Down in the workings, he set about placing a plank of wood against the bank as a target and standing about twenty feet away, he once again took aim and fired. Once again he missed, but he did seem to be a little nearer, this time missing it by only about a foot.

An hour and thirty rounds later, he finally hit the target and, just to prove that it was not just chance, he fired another six rounds and this time they all found the target. If nothing else, the exercise served to improve his morale somewhat.

Even though he was now satisfied that he had found his aim once again, he realized that hitting a stationary target was one thing but a moving target was an entirely different proposition. He knew that anyone he was likely to have to use a gun against would certainly not simply stand there and allow him to take aim. However, he had had enough for one day and since there was no great urgency and the fact that he could not afford to carry on wasting bullets at that rate, he turned his attention to food.

He looked at the strips of dried beef with a somewhat jaundiced eye and remembered the rabbit. Next time you won't be so lucky, he said to himself. Tomorrow I'll have rabbit stew.

Clay never had been much of a cook but his term in prison had taught him not to question too closely what the meal consisted of or how well it was cooked. However, his first attempt proved so underdone that even he had to leave it to cook for a lot longer. When he finally tasted it he decided that this time he had overcooked everything, burned the beans and had put so much salt in that it was almost inedible. However, eat it he did.

★ ★ ★

Clay did not eat rabbit stew the next day, or the day after that, but on the third day he did. Although pleased that he had finally hit a moving target and a very small one at that, he felt a little cheated.

A large eagle had swooped low overhead and dropped, talons open and wings spread wide, upon an unseen prey, unseen that was until it suddenly ran, squealing in terror from the tall grass the eagle had come down in. The rabbit raced straight at Clay, obviously not seeing him and Clay, who already had the gun in his hand, scarcely had time to take aim as he fired. The shot quickly silenced the screeching rabbit.

"Better luck next time!" he called to the eagle as it lifted itself into the air and he picked up the rabbit. "My need is greater'n yours." The eagle swooped low and Clay instinctively ducked as the bird flew off in search of another meal.

It was not until he set about gutting and cleaning the rabbit that he appreciated just how many flies there were around. There had been some in evidence before, but the smell of fresh meat had the effect of surrounding him in a buzzing, biting, black cloud. Relief came only when he dropped the dismembered carcass into the pot and hurled the remains as far away as he could. It was as he threw the guts and skin that he suddenly became aware of someone watching him. Instinctively he drew his gun but the stranger had placed himself well, directly in line with the sun.

Clay shielded his eyes and he heard the stranger laugh. "Son, if'n I'd wanted to kill you you'd've been buzzard meat ten minutes ago. Put that gun away, I'm comin' in."

The man was clever, he came forward ensuring that the sun still shone in Clay's face but eventually he was forced below the line of the sun and Clay could see an old, dirty, bedraggled figure who carried an ancient muzzle-loading rifle.

"Grizzly Evans!" exclaimed Clay. "Thought you'd've been dead years ago."

Grizzly Evans had been a local character for a good many years, coming and going as he pleased, walking everywhere. He had never been known to use a horse or mule and quite how he survived nobody seemed to know. Despite his unsavoury appearance, Grizzly Evans was trusted by everyone. He had never been known to take anything that did not belong to him nor did he ever ask for charity or hand-outs.

It was difficult to tell if, beneath the bearded features, the man was surprised or not, but he appeared to be.

"How'd you know my name?"

Clay smiled and his hand went to his face and he laughed. "I guess you don't recognize me."

Grizzly peered closely for a few moments. "Clay McKinley," he announced at length. "You was clean-shaven last time I saw yer, that threw me for a while." He moved to the fire and prodded the rabbit in the pot before sitting down. "Got any coffee?" he asked.

"Just finished the last," said Clay. "Won't take long to heat up some more though."

"Sure would appreciate some coffee," drawled Grizzly. "I ain't had me a mug of coffee in more'n . . . " He paused to consider. "Six weeks, must be that long. Yep, six weeks ago, out at Chepaquidic." He looked up at Clay for a moment, nodded and spat an unsavoury looking wad of something into the fire and smiled as it sizzled briefly. "Last I heard of you you was on your way to prison. You done your time already? I know time don't mean that much to me but didn't you get fifteen years? I'm darned sure it ain't been that long."

"No, I did three years," said Clay.

Grizzly nodded briefly and gazed into the fire. "I guess that means you was either proved innocent or you escaped."

"Escaped," said Clay.

"Figures," nodded Grizzly, once again spitting into the fire. "I reckon if you'd been found innocent there'd've been one or two faces missin' from Lewis, but they ain't."

Clay was interested. "Like who?"

The old drifter turned and studied Clay more closely. "I reckon you must be about the only man in Lewis who didn't know," he said. "Ain't no proof of course, they made sure all the proof was laid on you."

"So it seems," said Clay. "What do you know about it?"

"More'n most folk think," replied Grizzly. "Only thing was nobody bothered to ask me. Could've saved you a whole lot of trouble if'n someone had thought to ask me what I knew. That's the trouble with most folk, they think ole Grizzly is daft an' don't know nothin'."

"Why the hell didn't you come forward?" demanded Clay.

Grizzly stared at Clay for a moment. "You gonna make some coffee or not?"

Clay decided that the best thing he could do was make the coffee and share his meal with the old drifter. It was well known that Grizzly Evans could be as stubborn as any mule when he wanted to be but he usually mellowed after a meal.

An hour later, both men having eaten and now on their second mug of coffee, Clay once again raised the question of what it was the old man knew.

"Guess you could say I saw everythin' what happened," said Grizzly. "I was dossin' in the old stable what used to be alongside Bert Cummins' place, you remember him, corn merchant . . . " Clay grunted that he remembered and urged Grizzly to continue. "Well, I was in the stable mindin' my own business like I usually do. Bert always let me use the stable, said if the horses didn't mind why the hell should he." He laughed and spat into the fire again.

Clay was normally a patient man but he was anxious to hear what the old drifter had to say, especially since it could prove very important.

"What the hell happened?" he grated. "We all know you used the stable."

Grizzly looked at Clay and laughed. "You young uns is all the same. You gotta have everythin' all at once, none of you got time to stop an' look an' listen. You don't know just how much you is missin' by bein' in such a tearin' hurry. I'm comin' to what happened, you just wait."

Clay realised that losing his temper would be a complete waste of time so he just sighed heavily, lay back, closed his eyes and waited for Grizzly to continue his story.

"Like I say," continued Grizzly, "I was in the old stable . . . it ain't there no more, not since the railroad moved in. Biggest mistake the town ever made was havin' that stinkin' thing go through town." Clay almost screamed, but bit his lip. "Eight at night it was, I knows that 'cos old Jake, the blacksmith, allus left his shack at eight on the dot to go to the saloon. Anyhow, I seen old Jake leave just as I was beddin' down up in the loft when four men came in. I knew who they was of course, but it was plain they didn't know I was there."

"Who?" demanded Clay.

"I'm comin' to that," snorted Grizzly. "There you go again, allus rushin' things." Clay sighed and closed his eyes. "There was Turnbull, president of the bank — he's dead now 'course, died about two months ago." Clay indicated with a grunt that he already knew. "Then there was Jim Proud, Tom Walker an' that Hans Gerber feller . . ."

"Gerhart," corrected Clay, "Hans Gerhart."

"Yeh, that's the feller," conceded Grizzly. "German feller, speaks kinda funny. Anyhow, like I says, they didn't seem to know I was there 'cos they started talkin' about how they was goin' to rob the bank the next day. Can't remember everythin' they said, not now anyhow, but I reckon I could've at the time, if'n somebody'd taken the trouble to ask me."

"Why the hell didn't you tell the sheriff?" asked Clay.

"Guess I thought it was none of my

business." He laughed. "I sure didn't have no money in the bank so it didn't affect me. Anyhow, me an' Giles Wilson weren't exactly the best of buddies. You ought to know that better'n most, he was all for runnin' me out of town."

Clay grunted and had to admit that Giles Wilson and Grizzly Evans had never seen eye to eye and Giles was always ready to blame any petty theft on the old tramp.

"You should've told him," said Clay. "Or me."

Once again the old man laughed. "Sure I could've, but what would you have done? The one time I did tell you anythin' neither of you believed me an' when it didn't happen all you did was laugh at me an' call me names."

Clay nodded: the old man was referring to having claimed to have overheard a plan to rustle some cattle. At the time they had taken him at his word and staked out the ranch where it was supposed to take place. In the event nothing happened. Grizzly had always insisted that it did not happen because they had told somebody else who had told the rustlers.

"I think we would have taken notice of you," said Clay.

Grizzly snorted his contempt. "Doubt it, young feller. Sure, it's easy to say after all this time an' after what happened, but you'd never 've believed me if'n I'd told you at the time that Turnbull was plannin' to rob his own bank would you?"

Clay smiled and was forced to admit that it would have been hard to believe. "Is that all?" he asked.

"Ain't that enough?" asked Grizzly.

"It would be a whole lot more convincin' if you'd actually seen 'em do it?"

"Seen 'em do it!" laughed the old man. "Hell, there was a whole townful saw that, what difference would me seein' it've made?"

"Five people actually saw the raid," said Clay. "Me an' Giles Wilson was out of town at the time. Anyhow, everyone who did see it swears there was only three of 'em."

"Ain't surprisin'," said Grizzly. "It'd be hardly likely that Turnbull would actually rob his own bank. I hear he was there though, they tied him up an' then shot that clerk feller. I guess he saw who they were an' they had to kill him."

"Is that all?" Clay asked again, sensing that the old man was keeping something back.

A big grin spread across the bearded features. "No, as a matter of fact it ain't. I'd left town before dawn, headin' up here as a matter of fact. I often comes up here, it's peaceful an' folk don't come here too often. Ain't nothin' for nobody to come here for I reckon. Anyhow, like I say, I was up here when I heard horses so I hid in one of the old shafts."

"Why bother to hide?" queried Clay.

"That's 'cos I don't like folk all that much. Anyhow, I said I heard 'em not saw 'em. I was up in that shaft up there . . . He pointed up the side of the workings. "They rode in, an' I saw it was Proud, Walker an' Gerber." Clay did not bother to correct the old man this time. "They was carryin' sacks which they emptied out. Full of money they was. I ain't never seen so much money in my whole life. At the time it looked like they'd got all the money in the world . . . "

"Three hundred thousand dollars," said Clay, "give or take a few dollars. "Leastways that's what Turnbull claimed was missin'."

"That's more'n I ever seen before or since," grinned the old man. "Anyhow, they set about dividin' it into four. I know it was four 'cos they had six sacks an' they left two of 'em behind." He laughed again. "They left a handful of money in one of the sacks, just over a hundred dollars. Stuffed in a corner it was. That money sure was useful. I ain't one to spend much — never had that much to spend before — I sure had me a good time with that money though."

Clay smiled. "That makes you an accessory after the fact."

"Don't even know what that means," smiled Grizzly. "Ain't nothin' anyone can do about it now, I spent it all."

"And in the meantime I spent three years in prison," sighed Clay. "All because you didn't tell nobody."

"Son," said Grizzly, "I been on this earth a good many years an' I reckon the only reason I lived this long was 'cos I didn't get involved in other folks' business an' 'fore you ask, no, I ain't prepared to go to no sheriff an' tell him what I told you. Sure, I knows you was set up, that's one of the things I heard 'em talkin' about." He laughed again and spat into the fire and studied the flames for a moment. "I figured you was old enough an' clever enough to look after yourself. You had schoolin' an' all that, which is more'n I ever had, can't even write my own name. Mind, I ain't never had no need for readin' or writin'. Schoolin' don't teach you how to use a gun, track a rabbit or deer or know what roots an' grubs is good to eat out in the desert. Talkin' about knowin' how to use a gun, seems like you is a mite rusty. They used to reckon you was just about the best shot in the territory but I was watchin' you for a while an' I'd say you'd be best not lettin' on to anyone just how bad you are right now."

"I hadn't intended to," said Clay, "but you're right, I am kinda rusty. Three years in prison saw to that."

Grizzly smiled and nodded. "I was in prison once, in my younger days. I got one year for stealin'."

"Don't tell me," grinned Clay, "you didn't do it."

"Sure I did it," laughed Grizzly. "Ain't no arguin' with that. I stole me a rifle an' two apple pies."

"Two apple pies!"

The old man laughed. "Yep, two apple pies. They was standin' on the window ledge to cool when I broke in an' stole the rifle. I'd lost my own rifle in a game of cards. Real crooked game that was. They knew I was somethin' of a greenhorn an' I got cheated out of it. Anyhow, I came on this homestead where there was only a woman — her old man was in town or somethin' — so I took the rifle an' the pies . . . " He laughed loudly again. "Should've left the pies. They was just about the worst I ever tasted in my life. Anyhow I was caught an' sent to prison for a year."

"Which one?"

"Same one I hear you was sent to," replied Grizzly. "I was young an' fit then, but that place almost broke me. Only place I seen grown men cry or beg for mercy. Them prison guards was real mean, flog you if you so much as looked at 'em in a way they didn't like or you got on the wrong side of 'em in any way."

"They ain't changed much," nodded Clay.

"Then there was them queer fellers,"

continued Grizzly.

"Queer fellers?" asked Clay.

"Yeh, them what took to satisfyin' themselves with young fellers like I was."

Clay nodded, although he had not had any problems in that respect, he knew that younger men, especially those little more than boys, were subjected to the unsavoury attentions of some of the older and longer serving men and even one or two guards.

"So you've done time," said Clay. "If I get caught I'll be back for a whole lot longer than the fifteen years I was sent for. That's where your story could help. Let me take you to the governor, he's a good man, understandin' an' all that. He'll probably even make sure you get paid for your trouble."

The old man shook his head and once again spat an evil looking wad of tobacco into the fire and watched it splutter and sizzle. "Sorry, son," he said. "You is on your own this time. If'n they'd asked me at the time I probably would've said what I knew but they didn't an' it was three years ago. If'n this governor is so understandin' why don't you go see him yourself? You can tell him what I said, just don't expect me to testify or nothin' like that."

"Will you confirm what I say if I do?"

Grizzly laughed. "They reckon I'm daft, spent too long wanderin' in the sun. I'll just pretend I ain't got the faintest idea what the hell you is talkin' about."

"Thanks for nothin'," sneered Clay.

Grizzly seemed unabashed. "That's OK, son, at least you know what really happened."

"I already had a pretty good idea," said Clay, "you just filled in a few gaps."

"Best thing you can do now is keep on movin'," advised Grizzly. "What's done is done, ain't no way you is goin' get three years back. Now you is free just keep on goin'.

"I wish it were that simple," sighed Clay.

The old man laughed again. "Sure, it is that simple. You got yourself a horse an' maybe a few dollars in your pocket, what else do you need? You just sits astride that horse, point it in almost any direction that takes your fancy an' ride."

"There's certain people in Lewis who owe me!" grated Clay. "They owe me my reputation an' three years of my life an' I intend to collect my dues."

"An' get yourself killed while you is doin' it," said Grizzly. "I felt that way a couple of times myself but it soon passes."

"If that's what it takes," said Clay, "then so be it. I'll make sure I ain't the only one to go though."

"Turnbull beat you to it," reminded Grizzly, "an' I do hear that Jim Proud is back East somewhere."

"I've never been East," said Clay.

4

CLAY woke up early the next morning only to discover that Grizzly Evans had been up even earlier and had apparently continued his wanderings. The coffee pot was perched rather unsteadily on a stone by the fire but the contents proved to be fresh and hot and, after two cheroots and a good cough, Clay felt much better.

He had lain awake for what seemed like hours during the early part of the night, his mind constantly turning over all the possibilities but when sleep had finally come, he was still no nearer any decision. His thoughts had been interrupted by Grizzly's snores and in many ways Clay envied the old man and his freedom, although such a life would never suit him.

Although Grizzly had recognised him, Clay was reasonably certain that few others would, at least not immediately and he made a sudden decision to ride into Lewis and test his theory. Mick Hartford would be the only one, but he knew that he could rely on the store owner to keep his mouth shut.

★ ★ ★

At first, the sight of a bearded, unkempt stranger riding into Lewis did little more than attract the odd, disinterested glance and the rather more savage attentions of two dogs, although the owners of these soon called them to heel, glaring at Clay as if it were all his fault. Clay simply smiled and raised his hat in acknowledgement.

He had remembered Mick Hartford saying that the sheriff discouraged the wearing of guns and, not wishing to attract the attention of the law too soon, Clay had put his belt and gun in his saddle-bag.

It was almost midday and Clay had

a sudden desire to sample a glass of beer, something he had not tasted in over three years, although he had had whisky with Mick Hartford. He hitched his horse to the rail outside the nearest saloon and, after looking about to see if there was anyone he knew, slowly entered the dim, cool interior where he ordered a glass of beer.

The barman was a man he had known most of his life and, although he was given a strange look, it appeared that he had not been recognised. He sipped the beer, turned and looked around the room to see that there were only four other customers, three of whom he recognised and one stranger. Apart from giving him a brief glance, the men took no further interest in him and continued to play cards for pennies.

Clay was reasonably pleased: he had been a regular in this particular saloon in the past and had been on good terms with the barman so, after draining his glass, he decided that he would take a slow walk around the town and make a point of visiting places where he knew he might just be recognised. As things turned out he did not get beyond the door of the saloon.

★ ★ ★

"That your horse, mister?" demanded a young man displaying the badge of a deputy sheriff whom Clay did not recognise.

"Could be," he admitted. "Somethin' wrong?"

Two Indians dressed in jeans and buckskin shirts suddenly emerged from behind the horse and nodded to the young deputy.

Clay immediately realised that he had overlooked probably the most important factor in his decision to come to Lewis. Whilst people might not recognise him, horses were an entirely different matter and these men had instantly recognised a horse they had only recently broken.

"Seems to be some sort of difference of opinion," the deputy smiled sardonically. "You say this is your horse but these . . . er . . . gentlemen seem to think that it belongs to them."

Clay thought quickly. It was no use trying to claim that he had had the animal for some time since it was more than likely that the Indians could provide proof. Besides, the animal had only recently been shod and probably for the first time and all blacksmiths recognised their own work.

"The truth is," smiled Clay, "I found it wanderin' back there . . . " He nodded beyond the corrals. "Since he didn't have no brand, I figured he was a wild horse, leastways one that'd turned maverick an' I knows mavericks become the property of whoever finds 'em. Are you tryin' to tell me he wasn't a maverick?"

The deputy appeared to be taken off guard by this answer but he recovered quickly. "The saddle, where 'd you get the saddle?" he demanded.

"Now that is mine," replied Clay safe in the knowledge that that at least was true, even if Mick Hartford had given it to him. "My own horse died right under me a few days ago," he continued. "Anyhow, since when did Indians own horses? They don't earn that kind of money."

The deputy seemed slightly out of his depth. "Sure, I'll go along with that," he conceded, "but even they're allowed to round up mavericks an' they claim this is one they rounded up. Seems somebody opened the paddock an' let this an' some others out."

"An' are you suggestin' that that someone was me?" asked Clay.

"I ain't suggestin' nothin'," sneered the deputy. "I ain't takin' no sides either but these men do live an' work in these parts an' you're a complete stranger an' you obviously ain't come to Lewis on business, I knows a saddletramp when I sees one. I reckon the best way to sort this out is for you to explain to the sheriff."

81

Clay shrugged. "Sure, why not?" he agreed. It would be an opportunity to further test the ability of others to recognise him and it might just be a means of gaining further information. The deputy seemed rather surprised at the ready acquiescence of the stranger and allowed the gun he had been fingering rather nervously to drop back into the holster. Clay just smiled and led the way across the street to the sheriff's office.

"What about the horse?" demanded one of the Indians. "It belongs to me!"

The deputy turned and glared at the man. "Right now it don't belong to nobody," he hissed. "It stays right where it is until the sheriff decides."

"I'll take it back to the paddock," announced the Indian. "It is safer there."

"Are you deaf?" grated the deputy. "I said it stays right where it is until the sheriff decides who it rightly belongs to."

The Indian seemed rather sullen and spat on to the ground. "And he will decide it belongs to him . . . " He nodded at Clay. "Just because he is white and I am an Indian."

"I don't know what he'll decide," said the deputy. "Now are you comin' or not?"

Both Indians looked at each other for a moment and said something to each other which neither Clay nor the deputy could understand and suddenly kicked dust into the air and slouched off in the opposite direction.

Clay grinned. "Looks like I just won me a horse!"

The deputy was quite plainly well out of his depth and shrugged his shoulders. "Maybe you have, maybe you ain't," he said. "I ain't about to make a decision, Sheriff Turner can still sort it out."

"New to the job are you, son?" grinned Clay.

The deputy returned the grin and nodded sheepishly. "First week on my own," he admitted. "I ain't even had a drunk to deal with yet."

"At least you'll know what to do about folk who claim they found a horse," laughed Clay.

They mounted the boardwalk and Clay marched into the sheriff's office with a confidence honed with years of entering that same office and the marshal's office next door. Sheriff Joe Turner looked up from his desk, studied Clay for a moment and then looked past him at the deputy. His eyebrows raised questioningly.

"It seems we have somethin' of a dispute about the ownership of a horse," explained the deputy. "This feller was found with one of them horses that got out of the paddock the other day. He claims he found it wanderin' an' that his own horse had died, so he took it. Jimmy Two-Trees recognised it an' said it was rightly his."

The sheriff looked about questioningly. "So where's Two-Trees?"

"Seems he didn't want to come an'

get things sorted gut," said Clay.

"Is that right?" the sheriff asked his deputy.

"That's about the size of it," admitted the deputy. "I asked him — to come an' sort things out but he just didn't want to know."

"So what's your problem?"

"I . . . er . . . I guess there ain't one," faltered the deputy. "I just figured you ought to know what was happenin'."

"OK, so now I know," sighed Turner. "If Two-Trees can't be bothered to contest it, I guess that means this feller owns the horse." He smiled at his deputy. "You did the right thing, but you'll soon learn that Two-Trees an' most the others don't want to know when it comes to dealin' with the law. OK, Sam, back on the streets." He looked strangely at Clay for a moment. "You can stay here for a while."

"Am I bein' arrested?" asked Clay.

"Nope!" snorted the sheriff as his deputy left the office. "It's just that I like to know who the hell any strangers in town are an' what their business is."

"Is my name important?" asked Clay.

"I guess not," sighed Turner. "It probably wouldn't be your real name anyhow." He studied Clay a little closer. "I've got a good memory for faces an' there seems to be somethin' familiar about yours." He pulled a bundle of papers out of a drawer and flicked through them, occasionally glancing up at the man in front of him. "Nope, it don't look like there's a poster out on you but I can't help feelin' I have seen you somewhere before."

"I know the feelin'," smiled Clay.

"Have you ever been through Lewis before?"

"Once, a good few years ago," replied Clay. At least there was some truth in what he said.

"Mmmm . . . " mused the sheriff. "Don't think it was that. It'll come to me, it always does but since you ain't on the Wanted list an' Jimmy

Two-Trees doesn't want to challenge your ownership of the horse, I guess you can go. What are you in town for?"

"I guess you could say I had some unfinished business," grinned Clay.

Joe Turner looked slightly disbelieving. "Business! What kind of business could a man like you possibly have in Lewis?"

Clay just laughed, turned and opened the door. "I don't think you'd understand," he called back.

As he stood on the boardwalk, Clay felt quite pleased with the way things had turned out. Now he was the undisputed owner of a horse and, although he had half expected it, he had passed scrutiny by the sheriff and not been recognised — for the moment at least. Instead of returning to his horse, Clay wandered off down the street almost defying folk he met and whom he recognised to recognise him. The looks he received were certainly not ones of recognition but rather more of alarm.

He found himself, almost surprisingly, outside Mick Hartford's store and went inside. Mick was serving a female customer and absently said that he would not be long and suddenly looked at Clay with a mixture of surprise and great apprehension. Clay stood at the rear of the shop whilst the woman finished her business. Immediately Mick raced to the door, looked quickly up and down the street and slammed it shut and locked it, pulling down a blind.

"What the hell are you doin' back here?" demanded Mick.

"Now that's a fine welcome," laughed Clay.

"I know you an' me have always been good friends," hissed Mick, "but don't you think this is expectin' too much? How the hell would I explain to the marshal or the sheriff? I was kind of hopin' that the other night would be the last I would ever see of you, for your own sake, not mine."

"It's OK," said Clay, "I've just

been talkin' to Turner an' he didn't recognize me."

"You've what!" exclaimed Mick.

"I've just been talkin' to the sheriff," repeated Clay. "Seems that one of them Indians recognised the horse."

"I don't believe what you're sayin'!" Mick exclaimed again. "I would've thought your own common-sense would've told you they'd recognise the horse."

Clay laughed. "Yeh, it should've," he admitted. "Anyhow, that's got one thing sorted out, I now own the horse legally. The Indians just didn't want anythin' to do with the sheriff."

"OK, so now you own a horse," said Mick, plainly very upset at the arrival of Clay McKinley. "Now do yourself a favour an' get the hell out of here before someone does recognise you."

Clay slowly shook his head and smiled. "Sorry, Mick, I can't do that. I've got me one or two things to put right."

Mick threw up his arms in despair.

"May the good Lord give me strength!" he sighed. "I know you of old, Clayton McKinley and once that bull-headed mind of yours is made up I know there's almost nothin' that'll stop you. OK, go and do your damnedest. All I ask is that you don't involve me, don't make any social visits and don't expect me to attend your funeral."

"In other words keep out of your hair," laughed Clay.

"Precisely!" sighed Mick. "Now what the hell have you come here for anyhow? I'm sure it wasn't just to tell me you were still around."

"I thought you might be interested," said Clay. "I didn't really have anythin' in mind, but since you ask, I could do with some more bullets. I used quite a few learnin' how to use a gun again."

Mick pointed to a shelf behind the counter. "Take 'em!" he said excitedly. "Take as many as you need, I guess I can stand the loss. Just get the hell out of here an' don't come back."

Clay laughed and took two boxes of

a hundred in each box. "There was one person who recognised me almost straight away," he said.

"Who?" demanded Mick.

"Grizzly Evans," smiled Clay. "I met up with him out at the old silver mine."

"Then let's hope he don't show up in town," sighed Mick.

"I don't think you need worry about Grizzly," said Clay. "I reckon someone would be doin' Gerhart an' Walker a favour if they warned 'em I was on the loose."

"Like I said," sighed Mick, "I don't want to know. How you deal with them is your affair, just don't involve me."

"I won't," assured Clay. "Thanks for your help so far an' I promise I won't mention it to anyone."

The shop door suddenly rattled impatiently as someone tried to enter and Mick pointed through to the back and Clay obeyed. When he was certain that Clay would not be seen, Mick opened the door and apologized to the rather bemused elderly lady who complained that it was the first time she had ever known the store to be closed at that time of day.

★ ★ ★

In the alley which divided Mick Hartford's store from the new hotel and gaming saloon next door, Clay suddenly took it into his mind to pay the owner of the hotel, Tom Walker, a visit. He slipped the two boxes of bullets into his pockets, grinned to himself and boldly marched to the front of the building.

Inside, he found himself in a large room with many green baize-covered tables, a large spinning wheel and several machines along one wall each having long handles on the side. He had never seen machines like these before and idly pulled on one or two handles but nothing happened.

"All the way from New York, only got 'em last week," boomed

a voice behind Clay making him start. "The very latest in gamin' machines," continued the voice which Clay recognised as belonging to Tom Walker. "Ten cents is all you need to make 'em work," Walker boomed again. "Here, allow me to show you how." He took a coin out of his pocket and inserted it into a slot at the side. "Just put your ten cents in here an' then pull on this lever . . . " He pulled on the handle at the side and immediately a symbol which had been displayed behind a glass window span round and eventually ground noisily to a halt and a $ sign and the figure 2 appeared. Tom Walker laughed as a host of ten cent pieces clattered into a tray at the bottom of the machine. "Two dollars," he almost gloated. "Not bad return on ten cents."

"Is that all there is to it?" asked Clay, slightly bewildered.

"That's all," boomed Walker. "Just put your ten cents in here . . . " he indicated the slot — "an' take your winnin's from here."

"Sounds too easy," said Clay warily. "What's the catch?"

"Catch, sir?" said Walker as if he was offended. "There ain't no catch."

"You mean you win every time?" said Clay. "That don't make sense, you might as well stand at the door an' give money to everyone who comes in."

"Ah, yes," said Walker. "Well, of course you ain't guaranteed a win every time. That's the whole idea, chance. These machines are games of chance. Sometimes they pay out and sometimes they don't."

"I'll bet they don't pay a whole lot more than they do," smiled Clay.

"This *is* a gamin' house, sir," huffed Walker. "The house gotta make a profit too; how else could we stay in business?"

"That's more like it," smiled Clay. "How much can you win on these things?"

"All it costs is ten cents a time," said Walker puffing his chest out. "For that you can get anythin' from ten cents to ten dollars. Ten dollars is the most."

"I could use ten dollars," said Clay, dipping into his pocket and finding a ten cent piece. "I guess I can afford ten cents." He pushed the coin into the slot, pulled the handle and watched the disc behind the glass panel spin round. Much to Clay's delight and Tom Walker's disgust and horror, the disc clattered to a halt and displayed a $10 sign in the window. Immediately coins began to spill into the tray and Clay, whooping with delight, scooped the coins into his hat. Tom Walker put on a rather strained smile and immediately invited Clay to try his luck at some of the other tables. Even though it was midafternoon there were quite a few other players about, all of whom had heard Clay scoop the ten dollars and suggested that he buy everyone a drink. A young but heavily made-up woman approached and slipped her arm through his and informed him that she was a hostess and enquired if she could be of service in any way. Clay declined the offer to try his luck on other tables, made it plain that there were no free drinks and told the hostess — as politely as he could — that he was not interested in anything she had to offer.

The hostess stomped off swearing and Tom Walker pointed to a cashier's desk and told Clay he could change his winnings into more manageable currency. Clay took two five-dollar bills and then went to the bar. This appeared to please Tom Walker a little since he took it upon himself to serve, automatically reaching for a very expensive looking bottle of Scotch whisky. Clay smiled and declined the whisky and ordered a glass of beer.

"It ain't too many folk who just pocket their winnin's," said Walker with a hint of sarcasm in his voice. "I know ten dollars ain't much but to a man like you I suppose it must mean more'n it does to most."

Clay sipped at his beer, which he had

to admit was very good, and smiled at Tom Walker. "An' exactly what is a man like me?" he asked.

Tom Walker smiled weakly. "Well, it seems to me you ain't exactly a man of wealth. In fact I had you down more as a drifter, but them clothes look kinda new."

"That's 'cos they are new," said Clay. "I guess even drifter's gotta have new clothes sometimes."

Tom Walker just smiled and nodded. "I also hear that you stole a horse that Jimmy Two-Trees had just broken."

Clay looked sharply. "An' who told you that?"

"All over town," smiled Walker. "Two-Trees claims you stole it an' I hear tell you claim you found it wanderin'."

"If this Two-Trees is so darned sure I stole it, he should've gone along to the sheriff. He didn't so that means the horse belongs to me now."

Tom Walker laughed. "Don't get your hair off at me, it ain't none of my business. Only thing is I sure am glad to see someone put that Indian in his place."

"Which at a guess ain't in here," smiled Clay looking about.

"No, sir," smiled Walker. "No Indians, no blacks nor Mexican cowhands."

"Rich Mexicans are more'n welcome though," grinned Clay. Tom Walker did not reply. "Mighty fancy place you have here," continued Clay. "I was through here just over three years ago an' it wasn't here then."

"But neither was the railroad," Walker pointed out. "The town's changed a whole lot since then."

"For the better?" mused Clay. "Clay McKinley was sheriff here then. What happened to him?"

"Marshal," corrected Walker. "Clay McKinley was marshal an' Giles Wilson was town sheriff. You know McKinley then?"

Clay smiled. "You could say that I suppose. I don't reckon anyone knew him better 'n I did."

"But maybe you don't know he robbed the bank, killed a clerk an' was sent to prison for fifteen years," said Walker appearing slightly uncomfortable at discussing the matter.

"Yeh, I heard rumour," said Clay. "Only thing I am sure of is that Clay McKinley would never get himself involved in anythin' like that."

"Well the law says he was guilty," said Walker. "If the law says he was guilty then that's good enough for me. Anyhow, it really don't matter that much any more, word is that he was killed a few months ago. Somethin' about a wagon bein' washed into a river drownin' everybody."

Clay nodded. "Yeh, I heard that too. I guess there's one or two folk in this town sleepin' a little easier at night now."

"Meanin' what?" snapped Walker.

"Meanin' whatever you want it to mean," smiled Clay draining the beer in his glass. "Best beer I tasted in a long while. Thanks for the ten dollars. Maybe I'll be seein' you around."

"Maybe, maybe not," muttered Walker. "You sure seem mighty interested in Clay McKinley though."

"Could say that," conceded Clay. "I reckon you could say I have a personal stake in the matter, especially since I got me a witness who saw three men countin' out the money from the bank up at the old silver mine an' none of 'em was Clay McKinley."

Tom Walker's eyes widened and for a brief moment he was lost for words. "If . . . if that was the case, why the hell didn't he come forward at the time?"

"Could say he was never asked," replied Clay as he pushed himself away from the bar. He did not give Tom Walker time to say anything else but he knew that he had sown the seeds of doubt in Walker's mind and he fully expected some action.

Out on the boardwalk he was well aware that he was being watched through the large window of the gaming hall and was also aware that it was not Tom Walker alone. He sensed at least three pairs of eyes.

5

TOM WALKER almost crashed through the door to the sheriff's office and caused Sheriff Joe Turner and his deputy to grab briefly at their guns. When they saw who had created the noise they relaxed but stared questioningly at Walker.

"What the hell's got into you?" demanded Joe Turner. "Somebody win more'n they should've done?"

"Could say that," grunted Walker as he examined the door to see if he had damaged it. Satisfied that he had not, he straightened himself and walked over to the sheriff's desk. "I just had me a stranger at my place, big man, long hair an' full beard . . ."

"Sounds like the feller we had in over the horse," smiled the deputy. "There sure ain't no other feller with that description around town."

"Horse?" queried Walker.

"It don't matter none," said the sheriff. "So what's he done, robbed you?"

"Nope," conceded Walker. "Although he did win ten dollars out of one of them new gamin' machines . . . "

"There's always a first time for everything," laughed the deputy. "There ain't no law against that."

"That ain't the point," grumbled Walker. "There's somethin' about that feller what bugs me. I can't exactly put a finger on it but I reckon he's trouble."

"Somebody wins somethin' on one of them newfangled machines an' that makes him trouble?" asked Joe Turner.

"No, 'course not," Walker grumbled again. "In a way it's a good thing somebody did win ten dollars, it's good for business. Folk see somebody win an' they all start playin' thinkin' they're goin' to win too."

"Which they don't," laughed the sheriff.

"Sure they do," smiled Walker. "After he'd gone almost everybody tried their hand an' some won one or two dollars, but the profit from the machines more'n covered that. Besides, almost all of 'em ended up puttin' their money right back."

"So what's your problem?" asked the sheriff. "Seems to me this feller did you a favour by winnin'."

"No, it ain't that," sighed Walker. "There's somethin' about the feller I don't trust. Like I say, I reckon he's trouble. I get the feelin' that I ought to know him but I just can't place him."

Joe Turner nodded, this time agreeing with Tom Walker. "Sure, I know what you mean. First time I set eyes on him I had the feelin' we'd met before somewhere but for the life of me I can't think where."

"You too!" smiled Walker. "Who the hell is he, did he give any name?"

"Nope," replied Turner. "Didn't bother to push things on account of Jimmy Two-Trees didn't press the matter. It seems he was ridin' a horse Two-Trees claimed was his, a maverick he'd recently broken."

"Pardon me for askin', Mr Walker," said the deputy, "but you often get strangers in your place an' some win but most end up losin'. What's so special about this stranger?"

"Sure, I get lots of strangers an' most I wouldn't give a second thought to," said Walker. "I . . . I don't know, I can't explain it, it's just one of them feelin's."

"There's got to be more to it than just that," said the sheriff.

"Why?" asked Walker. "You admitted yourself that you had the feelin' that you ought to know him."

"That ain't the same thing," replied the sheriff. "What did he say or do to make you think he was trouble?"

Tom Walker looked a little uneasy for a moment but he cleared his throat and gulped slightly. "He seemed mighty interested in Clayton McKinley, said somethin' about havin' a personal interest in what happened."

Joe Turner studied the top of his desk for a moment and then looked up slowly at Walker. "An' why should that bother you? Clay McKinley's dead, that's official."

"Yeh, I know that," conceded Walker. "It's just that it makes me sort of uneasy when somebody comes around askin' questions after all this time."

The sheriff smiled. "I was only a deputy at the time, but I reckon I was one of the few folk in town who thought that Clay was completely innocent." He smiled knowingly at Tom Walker. "Why should some stranger askin' questions about Clay McKinley make someone like you nervous, Mr Walker?"

There was a certain menace in the sheriff's voice which made Tom Walker even more nervous. "No . . . no reason, I guess," he admitted. "I just thought that I'd better let you know how I felt, just like all good citizens should. We ain't had no real trouble in this town since the bank was robbed an' I just want to make sure it stays that way."

"Very civic minded of you, Mr Walker," smiled Turner. "I'll make sure that someone keeps an eye on him if he comes in again. Where'd he go by the way?"

"I didn't see," lied Walker. He and two men he employed to keep order in the gaming rooms had seen exactly where the stranger had gone and, as far Walker knew, one of them was still watching every move the stranger made.

The sheriff smiled and nodded. "OK, Mr Walker," he said. "I'll arrange for him to be watched, but there ain't a darned thing I can do unless he breaks the law in some way."

"You could find out who he is," suggested Walker.

"He probably wouldn't give his real name," said the sheriff. "And I've already checked all the Wanted posters an' he sure ain't among them. Nope, as far as I'm concerned there ain't a darned thing I can do."

"What about the town rule about no guns?" Walker suggested again.

"Maybe you didn't notice," smiled Turner, "but when I saw him he wasn't wearin' no gun. Anyhow, even if he was all I could do would be to tell him about the law an' providin' he left his gun somewhere that'd be the end of that. You ought to know that, we make sure all strangers deposit their guns either here or at the hotel."

Tom Walker thought for a moment. "Now you mention it, he didn't have no gun." He smiled slightly. "Why wasn't he wearin' a gun? He must've known about the rule."

The sheriff shrugged. "I've seen travellers who don't wear guns before, not many, I'll grant you that, but it happens sometimes."

"Well I've said my piece," said Walker. "I've got me a business to attend."

"Makin' sure nobody wins too often

on them machines of yours," grinned the deputy.

Tom Walker scowled but did not respond and stormed out of the office, calling to someone on the opposite side of the street as he left.

Sheriff Joe Turner looked thoughtful as he watched Tom Walker disappear and slowly stood up and walked to the window where he remained deep in thought for some time. Eventually he turned to his deputy.

"Go see if you can find this stranger, it might be worth having another word with him. Whoever he is, he sure spooked Tom Walker an' I want to know why."

"Bring him in you mean?" asked the deputy.

"Invite him," smiled the sheriff, "I don't think a man like him will take too kindly to bein' ordered."

"An' if he won't come?"

Joe Turner shrugged. "We'll wait an' see what happens."

The deputy departed and Turner

remained staring out of the window for some time, deep in thought when Giles Wilson, the US marshal appeared. Turner immediately opened the door and called Wilson inside.

"Hi there, Joe," grinned the marshal, "What's the matter with you? You look like you've got a problem."

"Not really," said Turner, inviting the marshal to sit down. "It's just that there's a stranger in town who seems to be upsetting a few folk."

He proceeded to tell the marshal what had happened so far. "It ain't really your territory," said Turner eventually. "As far as I can tell this stranger ain't done nothin' wrong, there don't appear to be any posters out on him an' apart from the incident with the horse there's no reason to even question him. I just wondered if you might happen to know who he is. I've sent Sam to ask him to come here."

"Ask?" queried Wilson.

"Sure, since I've got no grounds to arrest him, all I can do is ask."

"From the description," smiled Wilson, "he don't sound like no man I ever knew, apart from Grizzly Evans, but from what you say he's a much younger man. Mind you, a beard can hide an awful lot. I'll be in my office if you want me."

"Thanks Giles," said Turner. "There's just one more thing that's botherin' me but I don't suppose you know the answer any more'n I do. He must've said somethin' to Tom Wilson 'cos he sure seemed spooked. You got any ideas?"

"Now that you mention it an' since this stranger says he has a personal interest in what happened to Clay McKinley, and added to the fact that just before I came in here Tom Walker was ridin' off like a bat out of hell towards Hans Gerhart's place, I'd say a hornets' nest that's been dormant for three years has suddenly started to swarm."

"The bank robbery," mused Turner. "Yeh, that crossed my mind too an'

111

I know you always said Clay was innocent an' I seem to remember you tellin' me once that it was very strange how certain folk suddenly seemed to have plenty of money."

"I was convinced then an' I'm still convinced that Tom Walker, Jim Proud an' Pete Turnbull knew a darned sight more than they ever admitted. I had the feelin' that Hans Gerhart was involved, but he seemed to keep well out of it." The marshal looked thoughtful and smiled. "It'll be interestin' to see what happens. I've got me an idea. Sure, I'll take a look at this stranger, but without him knowin'. It could be that I know who he is, but probably not."

Joe Turner also smiled and nodded slightly. "I think I get your drift. Let him have his head an' see what crawls out of the woodwork."

"It's a long shot," conceded Wilson, "and it isn't goin' to help poor Clay none an' maybe we'll never be able to prove a thing against any of the others, but at least they'll know that we know what really happened."

"Do I still ask him to come an' see me?" asked Turner.

"Why not?" smiled Wilson. "You can always use Jimmy Two-Trees an' his horse as an excuse. Anyhow, I'll be next door if need be an' I'll keep a look out in case he does drop by."

★ ★ ★

"Excuse me, mister." Deputy Sheriff Sam Gates seemed almost apologetic as he approached the bearded stranger. "The sheriff would like a word with you, if you don't mind."

"What for?" grunted Clay McKinley.

"I ain't at liberty to say, sir," mumbled the deputy. "All I know is I've been sent to ask you to call by the office."

"Not to arrest me?" asked Clay.

"No, sir, why should I want to arrest you? As far as I know you ain't done nothin' wrong."

Clay smiled and patted the deputy

on his shoulder. "OK, son, I won't make things hard for you, I'll be right along as soon as I've finished this drink."

Deputy Sam Gates had found his quarry in the saloon, although he had looked in earlier on but someone had told him that they had seen the stranger go in shortly after. Sam nodded and left the saloon to tell his superior that his mission had been a success.

Joe Turner opened the door of the marshal's office next door to his own and told Giles that the stranger was on his way. He returned to his own office and waited. About five minutes later he saw the big, bearded man amble slowly across the street towards the office.

"You want to see me, Sheriff?" drawled Clay as he opened the door. "I ain't done nothin' wrong, I hope?" Clay had deliberately adopted a slow, easy, country way of talking in an effort to help his disguise.

"Not as far as I know," grinned

Turner. "It's just that I've been thinkin' about this business with you an' Jimmy Two-Trees an' the horse."

"What's to think about?" smiled Clay.

"Nothin', really," admitted Turner. "It's just that I'd like to have everythin' legal like, mainly so's there can be no come-backs on me, if you understand."

Clay laughed. "Sure, I can understand that. What you want me to do?"

"I've written out somethin' which gives you legal right to the horse an' clears me of any charge of favourin' you against Two-Trees." He pushed a piece of paper towards Clay who did not even bother to read it.

"Where'd you want me to sign?"

"Right there, alongside my name," said Turner. "Ain't you goin' to read it?"

"Readin' never was my strong point," lied Clay.

"I see you can write though," smiled the sheriff as Clay rapidly scrawled something that he claimed was his signature. When it was shown to Giles Wilson later, neither of them could decipher it.

"Is that all?" smiled Clay.

"That's all," nodded Turner," thanks for your help."

"No problem," grinned Clay, well aware that there was far more to things than the sheriff claimed. He had not been slow to notice Marshal Giles Wilson studying him as he crossed the street. He was interested to know if Giles had recognised him, but at that moment he was not prepared to ask. "Where's a good eatin'-house? I'm gettin' kinda hungry."

"Down the street, next to the bootmaker's, Kate's Tea Shoppe, sounds kinda corny an' she's not long over from England. Best food you'll find anywhere though."

As Clay left the office, he noticed that Giles Wilson was still at the window of his office and for a brief moment he was very tempted to wave, but managed to resist.

Kate's Tea Shoppe seemed completely out of place in the rough-neck town of Lewis, but it seemed to find considerable favour with the ladies of the town, about ten of whom were gathered inside going through the motions of playing the genteel ladies. Most of them looked rather alarmed as the large, bearded stranger ambled in and commandeered the only vacant table. Kate Robinson, as Clay discovered her full name was, appeared completely unabashed and, when asked about hot food, rattled off four or five items of which Clay recognised only one — beef steak. He ordered the beef steak.

The size of the piece of meat, potatoes, greens and carrots on the plate she placed before him belied the outwardly genteel nature of the place. Most of the ladies seemed to approve the size of the meal, declaring that it was good to see a man enjoying his food, but that they could never manage such an amount since they had to be careful what they ate.

By the time Clay had finally mopped up the last of the gravy with a piece of warm, new, bread, all the ladies had left. "Fine place you have here," sighed a well-filled and contented Clay McKinley. "Your husband is a mighty lucky man to have such a fine cook for a wife."

"Not so lucky," she said in a soft, English accent, "he died a year ago."

Clay felt his face redden. "Sorry 'bout that ma'am," he apologised. "I'm fairly new to these parts, leastways it's been a few years since I was last here an' you weren't here then."

"Just under two years," smiled Kate. "No need to apologise, these things happen and life has to go on. Now, can I get you anything else?"

"Ma'am," beamed Clay, "I couldn't force another mouthful, that was the best meal I've had in many a year. I reckon I could manage some coffee though."

Kate Robinson looked at him and

smiled. "If that's the best meal you've had for many years then you must have eaten pretty poorly."

Clay gazed up into her clear, blue eyes for a moment and felt himself redden. "It's true, ma'am, but then they don't serve good food in prison."

"Prison!" Apart from the very slight rise in the note of her voice, she showed no other outward sign of surprise or concern.

"It's a long story, ma'am," nodded Clay, "I won't bore you with the details, sufficient to say that I was sent to prison for somethin' I didn't do. Maybe one day you'll hear all about it."

"How mysterious!" she giggled. "Of course you didn't do whatever it was you were supposed to have done — if you follow me."

"Yeh, I suppose prisons are full of folk who didn't do anythin'," he smiled. "It don't matter none if you believe me or not."

"Of course it matters!" she scolded.

"It should always matter what anyone thinks of you."

"And what do you think of me?" smiled Clay.

This time it was Kate who blushed. "What can I possibly think of you?" she asked, turning her face away. "A few minutes in my dining-room hardly qualifies me or you to have opinions. I'll go and make your coffee." She disappeared quickly into the kitchen where she seemed to make more noise than was necessary.

Clay saw a mirror on the far wall and looked at himself for a moment, surprised that his bearded features should have had such an apparent influence on her. True, he was clean and the beard well brushed, but he was hardly what he would have called handsome. Kate returned with a large mug of coffee which she placed on the table and turned to him.

"My ladies use bone china cups and saucers but somehow I can't visualise you as a bone china and saucer man."

"You'd be surprised," grinned Clay, "although I've got to admit that the amount in one of them hardly seems worthwhile." He picked up the mug and slurped a mouthful and then wiped his wet beard and moustache on his sleeve and almost immediately apologised for his action. "In prison you don't have time to stand on niceties, if you don't drink it fast someone is liable to snatch it off you."

Kate cocked her head on one side, smiling slightly but not pressing the question of why he had been in prison. "Why do you keep that beard?" she asked. "I'm quite certain that you would look much better and certainly a lot younger without it."

Clay placed the mug back on the table and thoughtfully stroked his beard. "Sure, I'll shave it off, I nearly did a couple of days ago but for reasons which don't concern you — I don't intend that to sound rude or offensive in any way — it suits my purpose to keep it, for another few days at least."

"Even more mysterious!" she laughed. She clasped her hands together. "I can see it all," she continued a little dreamily. "Man sent to prison for something he didn't do, comes back in disguise to wreak vengeance!"

Clay gulped down the remainder of his coffee and decided that a hasty retreat was in order. "How much?" he asked.

Kate looked at him a little strangely. "One dollar," she said softly. Clay gave her the money and picked up his hat. "Mr . . . er . . . You never told me your name . . . " She paused as if expecting him to rectify the oversight but when he did not she continued, "I'm sorry, I should learn to mind my own business. My trouble is I talk too much. I apologise, I seem to have hit a raw nerve."

"I guess you could say that," mumbled Clay. "It'd sure give me pleasure to tell you all about it one day, but for now it's best left." He paused and looked appealingly at her. "Just one thing, ma'am," he continued. "I'd be more 'n grateful if you don't go puttin' your ideas into other folk's heads, not yet-awhile anyhow."

"What ideas?" she asked, seeming to be genuinely perplexed.

"The one about comin' back in disguise."

She suddenly smiled. "So there is something in it! Very well, I won't say a word to anyone — on one condition."

"Condition, ma'am?" he queried. "I ain't used to folk makin' conditions."

Her smile changed to a laugh. "Two conditions! The first is that you stop calling me ma'am and the second is that as soon as you are able, I want to hear everything you have to say. I'll even treat you to a free dinner."

Clay too laughed lightly. "The first part is easy to agree to. OK, what do I call you?"

"Kate," she smiled. "Everybody calls me Kate, all except the Reverend Cunningham, he insists on calling me Mrs Robinson, but then he never calls anyone by their Christian names. My real name is Kathleen but I hate being called that or Kath, so everyone calls me Kate."

"OK, Kate," smiled Clay, "it's a deal. There is just one thing; it is more than possible that I might not be able to get back to see you."

"Why?" she asked.

"Because it is quite likely that I may end up dead."

The smile faded from her face and her fingers gripped together. "Then I suppose I shall just have to take that chance," she said a little hoarsely.

"Would it matter all that much?" Clay asked.

Kate scooped up the mug and a stray plate, turning her back on him. "No . . . no, I don't suppose that it would. After all, I do get quite a few strangers in here. Why should it bother me if one or even all of them get themselves killed?"

"Just thought I'd better let you know," Clay said softly as he turned and let himself out on to the street. He thought he heard the smashing of crockery behind him but he did not look back.

* * *

Marshal Giles Wilson looked as though he had great worries on his mind, a fact which did not go unnoticed by Town Sheriff Joe Turner as Turner entered the marshal's office.

"Did you see him?" asked Turner.

"Yeh," replied the marshal absently, "I saw him OK."

"And?" prompted the sheriff.

Giles Wilson looked up sharply, too sharply and Turner knew immediately that something was wrong. He waited for the marshal to say something which eventually he did.

"Ain't never seen the feller in my

life," Giles said slowly.

"I thought you'd say that," said Turner. He paused for a moment as the marshal lowered his face to look at the desk again. "Is somethin' botherin' you, Giles?" he asked.

"Wha . . . what? Botherin' me?" faltered Giles. "Why should anythin' be botherin' me?"

"You sure look like somethin' is."

"Well there ain't!" snapped the marshal.

"And you ain't never seen that stranger in your life before?" urged Turner. "Is somethin' botherin' you about him?"

The marshal stood up sharply, his heavy chair scraping back along the floor boards. He picked up a bundle of papers and tapped them into a neat pile on the desk top. "I told you, I ain't never set eyes on the man. How many times do I have to tell you?"

Joe Turner stepped back and raised his hands chest high. "OK, OK, keep your hair on. I believe you, you ain't never seen him before. Do we still just sit an' wait to see what he does an' what happens?"

Giles seemed to be on the point of saying something to the sheriff, but instead he just nodded his head and stared at the desk top once again. Joe Turner decided that the time was not yet ripe to press the matter further and left the marshal's office for his own where he called his deputy over.

"Sam," he said, "I want you to make it your business to find out everythin' you damned well can about that stranger. I want to know every move he makes, where he goes, who he talks to an' what about an' I even want to know every time he farts or wipes his arse. Until I say otherwise he is to be your sole job. Got that?"

"Got it," replied Sam. "Do I get to know what this is all about?"

"All you need to know is that . . . " He had been going to tell him about Giles Wilson. "No, you already know all there is to know. Just keep me informed."

"Do I follow him if he leaves town?"

"You follow him if he climbs up a cow's arse!" snapped Turner.

Sam Gates got the message!

6

KATE ROBINSON was tempted to cross the street when she saw the bearded stranger approaching but she gritted her teeth and was prepared to walk by with nothing more than a brief nod but even that resolve evaporated when they were face to face. Clay raised his hat, nodded his head and smiled at her.

"I see you are still alive," she said, trying her best to sound disinterested.

"So far," he grinned. "How long for is another matter."

"Well it certainly doesn't seem to bother you," she replied, standing to one side to allow people to pass on the boardwalk. "I wasn't sure if I believed you or not, but since you left my place I have had two visitors, both demanding to know everything you said."

"And did you tell them?"

She blushed and turned her head to look across the street. "Of course not. I mean, you didn't tell me anything did you, not even your name."

Clay too glanced across the street and saw Deputy Sam Gates idly leaning against a wall pretending that he was not interested. "Was he one of them?" he asked her.

"Him and a man who works for Mr Walker," she nodded. "For a seemingly harmless stranger you certainly appear to have upset quite a few people."

"One of my more likeable qualities," he grinned.

"And there's the other one," she nodded briefly, indicating someone behind him. Clay did not turn round. "His name is Victor Smith. He is employed by Mr Walker and has a reputation as something of a hard man. His main job seems to be to persuade people to pay their debts when they lose more than they can afford at the gaming tables. I'd be very wary of him."

"Thanks for the warning," said Clay. "Right now though, I think the less you have to do with me the better, for your own sake."

"I'll say amen to that," she said curtly. "All I can do is wish you the best of luck. I have no idea just what is going on and at this precise moment I do not want to know. Good day to you." She brushed quickly past him which gave him the opportunity to turn, pretending to watch her but in reality looking at the hard Victor Smith.

Smith was certainly not a man Clay recognised, but then since the coming of the railroad the town had grown and there were a great many people he did not know. His first impression was that Smith was indeed a mean-looking man who could probably make very good account of himself in any brawl. How good he was or indeed how ready he was to use a gun was something still to be tested.

Smith obviously said something to

Kate as she passed him and apparently received a very acid reply which he did not seem to like. By the time he turned his attention back to Clay, Clay was already crossing the street, heading for Deputy Sam Gates.

"You ain't the only one who's followin' me," he said as he mounted the boardwalk alongside the deputy.

"I beg your pardon, sir?" said Gates.

"I said you ain't the only one who is following me," Clay repeated.

"Following you?" queried Gates.

"It's no use pretending you ain't," said Clay. "If you want to know anythin', why don't you just ask me?"

"I'm sure I don't know what you're talking about," protested the deputy. "Anyhow, who else is following you?"

"So you admit you are," smiled Clay.

"I admit nothing," Gates protested again.

"OK, have it your way," sighed Clay. "Just for your information, the other feller is someone called Victor

Smith, I understand he works for Tom Walker."

"And why should he be following you?" asked Gates.

"Why not ask him?" Clay smilingly suggested. "Right now I'll save you a lot of bother. I'm leavin' town, just for the night you understand and where I'm goin' it's pretty open country so I'll be able to see if anyone follows."

"Where you go is none of my concern," said the deputy.

"Make sure your boss knows that too," said Clay with just a hint of threat in his voice.

He went along to the stables where he had left his horse for the day, paid for its keep and rode out of town just as the first signs of dusk were developing.

★ ★ ★

"Haven't you got no sense at all?" growled Hans Gerhart. "I suppose you think nobody saw you ride out of town?"

"I often come out here," objected Walker.

"But not riding as if the Devil was on your heels," said Gerhart. "It was probably just what this stranger wanted you to do, just to prove to himself that he was right."

"Yeh," muttered Walker. "Maybe I should've given it more thought, but I wanted to let you know as soon as possible. He does reckon he has a witness who saw us out at the old mine with the money."

"That was more than three years ago!" hissed Gerhart. "If that was the case why didn't whoever it was come forward at the time?"

"How should I know?"

"Precisely, my friend," smiled Gerhart. "Personally I think that this stranger just said that and just happened to choose the right place. All he wanted to do was frighten you and I must admit that he has succeeded."

"I still don't like it," grumbled Walker. "I've got me this feelin' that we ain't heard the last of things."

"And what do you suggest we do about it?" demanded Gerhart.

"I don't know, I ain't really thought about it."

"Just as you didn't think about coming out here. I'm surprised that you have not suggested having him killed."

"That'd be stupid," declared Walker. "That'd involve someone else and that's somethin' we can't afford."

"Now you are talking sense," said Gerhart. "If and only if it is necessary that he should die then one of us must do it."

"I ain't no killer," objected Walker. "That's more your department, it was you who killed the clerk."

"Because he recognized me," Gerhart pointed out. "It was necessary."

"Then you'd better start thinkin' about if it's necessary this time," said Walker.

"Which is all very well if he was just calling your bluff and there is no witness. If there is, then we need to know who it is."

"See!" exclaimed Walker almost triumphantly. "You admit that he could be trouble."

"I have not denied it," said Gerhart, "but I am not prepared to be panicked into doing anything. The law is on our side. Clayton McKinley was convicted of the robbery over three years ago. Now he is dead so there is nothing to fear from him. It is up to this stranger to prove that we did it. Turnbull is dead so there's no chance of him talking. Jim went back East somewhere and he cannot afford to talk so that leaves just you and I."

"I'm having him followed," said Walker. "I put Vic onto it."

"Then take him off!" ordered Gerhart. "If this stranger is as clever as he seems to be then it will not take him long to realize that an oaf like Smith is following him. Now I suggest that you get back to town and look after your hotel and continue to act as if nothing is wrong. I know it will be difficult for you, you always did panic too easily."

★ ★ ★

"Maybe it wasn't such a good idea after all," muttered Joe Turner when his deputy told him what had happened. "OK, forget all about it. The trouble is he now knows we're interested in him. In the meantime I'm going to have a talk with Tom Walker."

Deputy Sam Gates considered himself quite bright and smiled smugly. "I was thinkin' that if this feller claims to have a personal interest in Clay McKinley, maybe he was in prison with him. I think it ought to be checked out."

The sheriff opened a drawer and pulled out a telegraph message. "Already done," he said. "There's only two people who were in contact with McKinley in prison who have been released. The others were either killed in the accident or are still there." He handed the telegraph message to his deputy who seemed rather downcast.

"James Barrymore, also known as Humpy Barrymore because he has a deformed back and Pablo Menengez," he read.

"Which rules that idea out," said the sheriff. "It was a good idea though an' don't take it too hard that someone else thought of it before you did. That's life an' somethin' you have to learn when you are a lawman."

"Then who is he?" asked Sam.

"That's somethin' I think Giles Wilson knows," said the sheriff, quietly. "He left town almost as soon as he'd seen the stranger cross the street. I talked to him straight after and then he left. He said somethin' about urgent business with the governor."

"The governor?" said Gates. "That's almost a two-day ride an' hard ridin' at that."

"Well there was somethin' about the man which sure seemed to bug Giles," said Turner. He sighed and pushed himself back in his chair and clasped his hands behind his neck and stared at the ceiling. "Just what the hell is it about this stranger which sends a hotel owner runnin' scared an' makes a US marshal run for the governor?"

"Have you thought about Mick Hartford down at the general store?" asked Gates, expecting to be rebuffed yet again.

"Hartford?" asked the sheriff.

Sam Gates was quite pleased that at last he had made a suggestion which had not already been thought of. "Sure, from what I heard Mick Hartford and Clay McKinley were great buddies. Maybe he knows who the stranger is too."

Joe Turner smiled, allowing his deputy a rare moment of glory. "Now why didn't I think of that," he nodded. "Good idea, Sam, you're learnin' fast." He decided to allow Sam to bask in his glory a little longer. "Why don't you go on down there an' find out. He's bound to have seen him about."

"Yes, sir!" said Sam gleefully. He

could hardly get out of the office fast enough.

The sheriff saw Tom Walker ride back into town and slowly ambled across to the hotel, not wanting to cramp his deputy by making it seem he was checking on him since the hotel was next door to Mick Hartford's store.

★ ★ ★

"It was just a thought, Mr Hartford," said Sam Gates almost apologetically. "It's well known that you an' Clayton McKinley were great friends which made me think that just maybe you might know who this stranger is. He sure seemed interested in what happened to Mr McKinley."

Mick Hartford was wary but he tried not to show it. "Sure, it was no secret that Clay an' me were friends an' I probably knew him better'n anyone else but I've never met this stranger before."

"You've seen him then?"

"Twice," said Mick. "He came into the store to buy some supplies."

"And you have no idea who he is?"

"I said I'd never met the man before," said Hartford. "That don't mean I don't have some idea about who he is . . . "

"You *do* know him!" exclaimed Sam.

"Nope," smiled Hartford. "I've never set eyes on him before. I think he just might be Clay McKinley's brother."

"Brother!" exclaimed Sam. "I never knew he had a brother."

"I don't think you knew Clay McKinley," smiled Mick. "How old are you, Sam?"

"Just eighteen," replied Sam.

"Which would make you less than fifteen when Clayton McKinley was US marshal."

"Sure, but I seen him around," objected Sam.

Sheriff Joe Turner stared at his deputy with a mixture of disbelief and admiration. Disbelief in that he too had never heard of Clayton McKinley having a brother and admiration that his deputy had at last come up with something.

"Giles Wilson would know," he declared. "Apart from Mick Hartford, Giles probably knew Clay better'n anyone. The trouble is he ain't here to ask. Still, it would account for why some folk thought they ought to know him. I never knew Clay all that well myself and I've no idea if he had a brother or not."

"So what do we do now?" asked Sam.

"Precisely nothin'," smiled Turner. "I went to see Tom Walker but couldn't get any sense out of him. He wouldn't say anythin' that we don't already know, but I think he's hidin' somethin'. One thing's certain, he's runnin' scared."

It was dark and moonless when Clay reached the old silver mine and he was put on his guard when he was greeted by the warm glow of a fire but a brief glimpse of a dark silhouette confirmed that it was Grizzly Evans.

On the way, Clay had stopped frequently to check if he was being followed but it appeared that both Sam Gates, the deputy sheriff and Victor Smith had abandoned the idea. In a way, Clay was disappointed that Smith had not followed him, he would have enjoyed questioning the man.

"Thought it was about time you was back," grunted Grizzly as Clay unsaddled his horse. "You hungry?" Clay said that he could eat something. "Rabbit!" declared Grizzly. "I managed to catch two."

Clay thought about the meal he had had at Kate's Tea Shoppe and glanced at the bloodied carcasses of the rabbits already skewered over the fire and his stomach protested slightly. "How'd you get on in Lewis?" continued Grizzly. "Anyone recognise you?"

"A few thought they should know me," said Clay, "but they didn't seem to tie me up with a man they think is dead."

"No reason why they should," said Grizzly. "Most folk is very trustin', "specially when the law says somethin' an' if the law says you is dead, then as far they're concerned you is dead."

"I got Tom Walker worried though," grinned Clay. "I told him there was a witness who'd seen someone countin' the money out here. It sure seemed to have some effect 'cos he hared off out of town. I can't be certain where he went but I reckon it was to Hans Gerhart."

Grizzly looked up sharply. It was difficult to tell if he was alarmed, annoyed or both, partly because of the light, partly because of his beard but mainly because Grizzly nearly always seemed to look annoyed.

"You told him I saw?" he demanded.

"Never mentioned you," Clay tried to assure him. "I just said there was a witness."

"It won't take 'em long to put two

an' two together," muttered Grizzly. "Damn fool thing to do. I knows you was a marshal, but I don't wanna be involved. If anyone asks me, I don't know what the hell you is talkin' about."

"I don't see why anyone should think it was you," said Clay. "I didn't even hint at it."

Grizzly seemed to scowl beneath his beard and the warning flash in his eyes was plain even for Clay to see in the firelight. "Gerhart ain't no fool," he said. "Drifters come an' go but none of 'em ever seem to come back. He'll soon work out that the only man likely to be around an' still around is me. Maybe I should leave right now."

There was no doubt that Clay had annoyed the old man and whilst he felt guilty about it in one way, in another he felt that if it forced either Gerhart or Walker or both to act, it was a price worth paying. Grizzly was quite right about one thing, Hans Gerhart was no fool.

* * *

"Good morning, Mrs Gerhart," greeted Kate Robinson as the rather portly figure almost waddled into the tea shop. "We don't see you in here very often."

"Hans has some urgent business in town," huffed Gwendoline Gerhart. "I told him that if he had business, the least he could do was bring me in. I haven't been in town for more than three weeks." She looked around the room and smiled at two other ladies already sipping cups of tea. "Good morning, Mary, Anne." She nodded at them. "Do you mind if I join you?" She did not wait for an answer before dumping her huge buttocks on to a rather flimsy looking chair at the table. The chair groaned slightly but managed to withstand the sudden onslaught.

The ladies — Mary and Anne — seemed rather dismayed at the prospect of sitting at the same table as Gwendoline Gerhart, but they smiled weakly and raised no objection other than a sharp, resigned glance at Kate. Kate simply smiled knowingly back and went to get another pot of tea, a china cup and another plate of cakes and cookies. Gwendoline Gerhart's appetite for such things was almost legendary.

"I've been looking at the material and dresses in Jane Sherwood's," Gwendoline announced. "Really, it's a wonder that woman does any trade at all, she had nothing in my size and I'm quite certain that material was the same as she had last year. You'd think she would cater for the average-sized person wouldn't you? Mind you, she probably makes more money out of dress making than selling ready-mades."

It took all of Mary and Anne's will-power to suppress a smirk at the idea of Gwendoline Gerhart being average size. Further embarrassment was saved as three other ladies entered the shop. At first they looked in dismay at the huge figure which greeted them but then they smiled almost in sympathy at Mary and Anne as they seated themselves at another table.

"That young man seems to have created quite a stir," said one of the new arrivals, Grace Talbot, probably the oldest resident of Lewis and to whom all men were young these days.

"What young man?" asked Kate as she served them with obligatory china teapot, cups and plate of cakes and cookies.

"The one you took such a shine to!" chided Mrs Talbot. "The one who was in here yesterday, the one with the beard." She shivered in an exaggerated manner. "I can't stand beards, they're most uncomfortable at times and they only make a man look a lot older than he is."

"Uncomfortable?" queried one of the other ladies.

Mrs Talbot laughed. "No need to be prissy in here," she laughed. "You know exactly what I mean."

"I'm sure I don't," objected the

woman. "My Tom has never had a beard."

Grace Talbot laughed again. "No, your Tom hasn't, but that man from the railroad company who was here last year did."

Cissy Walker blushed brightly and busied herself with the teapot whilst the remainder of the company smirked knowingly at each other. Even Kate Robinson found it difficult to suppress a smile.

"In what way has this young man caused a stir?" asked Kate, not bothering to deny that she had indeed taken a shine to him as Grace Talbot put it.

"They do say he is Clayton McKinley's brother," continued Mrs Talbot. "Come to take revenge on his brother being sent to prison."

Gwendoline Gerhart turned in her chair in an attempt to face the other ladies. "I don't know what it was all about, Hans never tells me anything, but your Tom came to see us last night. He looked very worried and for the rest of the night I couldn't get a civil word out of Hans and this morning he announced that he had to see your Tom."

"That would explain Tom sending me out with some money and instructions to buy what I wanted for myself and not to disturb him before noon," said Cissy Walker. "I was too surprised to ask him what it was all about. After all, it isn't often that any man puts his hand in his pocket willingly so I thought I'd better take advantage while I could. Anyway, he's called that dreadful man Smith in as well."

Grace Talbot sniffed knowingly. "I wonder if the sheriff or the marshal have looked closely into that man's background. I don't suppose for one moment they have or I think they would have found that they had a murderer in town."

"Murderer!" gasped the other ladies.

"That is what I firmly believe," pronounced Mrs Talbot. "I don't think there is any need for any of us to worry though, he's got a good job and won't want to upset the law too much. Yes, he may be a bad one but we're all safe enough."

Further conversation was interrupted as another four ladies entered and for a few minutes there was a babble of chatter as the newcomers were brought up to date on the latest gossip. When the noise eventually subsided, one of the newcomers suddenly announced, in a very important voice: "I don't want to sound alarmist and of course you will understand that I'm not accusing anyone of anything, but I think this Mr Smith is out to kill this stranger, Clayton McKinley's brother or whoever he is!"

"For someone who doesn't want to sound alarmist, I'd hate to be around when you did," said Mrs Talbot. "What on earth are you talking about?"

The woman hunched forward confidentially. "Well," she almost whispered, "my Daniel says he overheard Smith talking to another man in the saloon last night — not that Daniel makes a habit of going into such places you understand . . . " The ladies nodded their understanding while at the same time giving each other knowing nudges and little grins. "Well," she continued, "he heard Smith tell this other man to find out where the stranger went at night because it looked like he would have to deal with him . . . "

"Deal with him?" said Mrs Talbot. "Is that all?"

"What more do you want?" huffed the storyteller. "When a man like Smith says he has to deal with someone it can only mean one thing. I remember Smith threatening to deal with Cecil Graham about six months ago and just afterwards they found poor Cecil dead in his barn with a broken neck."

"He got trampled by a horse," said Gwendoline Gerhart. "There was no doubt about that. Mr Fraser, the veterinarian even found blood on the horse's hoof and Doctor Trimble said the injuries were in keeping with being trampled."

"Well I thought at the time it was too much of a coincidence," insisted the woman, "and I still think so."

"Smith is employed by my husband!" grated Cissy Walker. "Are you implying that my Tom has told Smith to kill the stranger?"

"I'm implying nothing," hissed the woman harshly. "All I know is what my Dan told me and he never tells me lies."

"Only when he's drunk!" snarled Gwendoline Gerhart. "I resent the implication too since my Hans has regular business dealings with Tom Walker. Hans would never be party to anything underhand or illegal."

"It really is a scandalous thing to say," Cissy Walker almost screamed. "You can't go around accusing innocent people of planning murder, but then it's typical of you Joan Gibbs, you always were too ready to let your tongue and your imagination run riot."

"I'm only telling you what was told to me," defended Joan Gibbs.

"Your trouble is that you only hear what you want to hear," raved Cissy Walker. "I know you're saying this just to get back at my Tom. It was well known that after your first man ran out on you and before Daniel came on the scene that you were doing your best to get my Tom into your bed. Just because you never succeeded you have been trying to blacken his name ever since."

Joan Gibbs smiled almost contentedly. "How do you know I didn't succeed?"

The gathering broke up amid near pandemonium and a fight was only narrowly averted when Kate Robinson called in the passing and unfortunate Deputy Sheriff Sam Gates.

7

"WHAT the hell was that all about?" asked Sheriff Joe Turner when his deputy returned to the office after eventually calming the ladies.

He and most of the townsfolk had been witness to the antics of the ladies as they tumbled out of Kate's Tea Shoppe and a few had even been heard to urge both Cissy Walker and Gwendoline Gerhart into further action.

"I'm not at all certain," sighed Deputy Sam Gates. "I couldn't get no sense out of any of 'em, 'ceptin' maybe Kate herself. Somethin' about Joan Gibbs an' Tom Walker an' Vic Smith bein' told to murder someone."

"Murder!" exclaimed the sheriff. "Murder who?"

Once again Sam sighed and wiped

his forehead on his sleeve. "From what I could gather it must have been this stranger. Don't ask me the details, I'd rather handle a couple of mountain lions than even one of them women."

"All part of the job," smiled Turner. "Still, somethin' pretty serious. I know they meet regular at Kate's an' most go 'cos they know if they don't it'll be them what's pulled to pieces. First time I've ever seen 'em come to blows though."

"Time was when we had a nice, peaceful town," said Sam nodding in the direction of Kate's Tea Shoppe. "Then *he* turns up." The stranger was at that moment riding into town and was alongside Kate's when she suddenly rushed out and spoke to him. "The man hasn't even done a thing," continued Sam, "but he sure has succeeded in stirrin' just about everybody up. Do you think he is Clay McKinley's brother?"

"Best way of findin' out is to ask him," said Turner. He waited until the stranger was alongside the office and called out to him, telling him he wanted to talk. The stranger smiled and nodded, dismounted and tied his horse to the rail.

"Mornin', Sheriff, Mr Deputy," he said as he mounted the boardwalk. "I hear you've been havin' problems with the ladies."

"Probably all thanks to you," huffed Sam.

"Me!" laughed Clay. "How the hell could you put that down to me? I wasn't even in town."

"It seems to me that you don't have to be anywhere or do anythin'," said Joe Turner, "but trouble ain't been very far behind you wherever you've been."

Clay shrugged and smiled. "Just my charming personality," he said. "So what can I do for you, Sheriff?"

"You can start off by telling me just who the hell you are."

"Nobody who matters," smiled Clay. "You could say I'm just a nobody."

157

"Mick Hartford reckons you could be Clayton McKinley's brother," said Sam Gates. "Are you?"

Clay smiled knowingly. "As far as I know, Clay McKinley never had no brother. I think there's a sister somewhere, Phoenix was the last place I heard she was. No, sir, I ain't Clayton McKinley's brother but just who I am I ain't sayin', not for the moment at least."

"You seem to know an awful lot about Clay McKinley," said Turner. "How come?"

Clay shrugged. "That's my business but you could say I know more about him than anyone else ever could."

"OK, so you won't say and I guess I can't force you since you ain't done nothin' wrong — yet." He sighed heavily and banged the desk with his clenched fist. "That's just the problem, you ain't done nothin' wrong but you sure have upset a whole lot of folk."

"An' I aim to upset 'em even more before I'm finished," snarled Clay.

"Maybe when I've done what I set out to do you'll find out who I am. All I can say is what I told Tom Walker: I've got me a witness who saw Tom Walker, Hans Gerhart an' Jim Proud countin' a whole heap of money just after the robbery."

"Witness!" exclaimed Turner. "What witness?"

"You'll find out in time," said Clay. "For the moment that's all I'm prepared to say 'ceptin' that it seems someone is out to kill me."

"Vic Smith?" said Sam.

"He's just the means of killin' me," said Clay. "I'd be lookin' to Tom Walker an' Hans Gerhart."

Sheriff Joe Turner sat back and smiled. "As a matter of fact I'm ahead of you but why the hell should I bother? This town don't owe you nothin'. We had a peaceful set up before you came along. I reckon most folk in Lewis wouldn't give a damn if you was shot dead right now."

"You're probably right about them

not givin' a damn," agreed Clay, "but this town owes me more'n you could ever imagine." He stood up and went to the door. "Now, if you ain't got no more stupid questions I've got some unfinished business." He opened his saddle-bag and took out his gunbelt which he proceeded to fasten round his waist. "I know all about your town rule about not wearin' a gun but my life has been threatened and a man does have the right to defend himself."

"The same rule applies to everyone, includin' you," snorted the sheriff. "Unless you want to spend a few days in jail you'd better take that off right now."

Clay sneered and squared up to the two men. "And which one of you is man enough to arrest me or take this gun off me?" He jerked his head backwards indicating something across the street. "That's Smith across the street and I'd say that he's got a gun hidden under that jacket. That's a winter coat; what's he doin' wearin' it in this heat?"

"You're just guessin'," snarled Turner.

"Just guessin' has saved my life on more'n one occasion," said Clay. "I ain't about to stop guessin' now."

Deputy Sheriff Sam Gates had casually taken hold of his rifle and now swung it up to waist height and aimed steadily at Clay. "I reckon I'm man enough to arrest you," he hissed.

Clay did not look at all surprised, instead he just laughed and continued to tie the thigh strap of the holster around his upper leg. "OK, son," he laughed. "You've got the drop on me. It doesn't make any difference though, I'm mountin' this horse and going about my business. The only way you can stop me is to squeeze that trigger. Can you do that? Can you shoot a man in cold blood, especially with all these witnesses? Go ahead, son, make a name for yourself."

The challenge clearly unnerved the deputy who licked his lips and glanced at his superior for guidance. Joe Turner, realising the haplessness of the situation indicated that he lower the gun.

"Since it appears that you're not stayin' in town," said Turner, "I guess that makes it OK to wear your gun. I don't know what your business is but you could save yourself a whole heap of trouble by keepin' well out of Lewis."

"Trouble is my middle name!" scorned Clay as he mounted.

He reined his horse round and rode out of town, this time a lot faster than he had ridden in.

★ ★ ★

The meeting between Hans Gerhart and Tom Walker had also been a stormy one. Vic Smith had been briefly called in and given instructions to locate Grizzly Evans. Smith had seemed surprised but did not question his instructions — he very rarely did. The meeting had continued amid protestations by Tom Walker that things were rapidly getting out of hand.

"Perhaps I should remind you that it was you who panicked first," sneered Gerhart. "The thing is Grizzly is the only man who could possibly have seen us."

"And what do we do with him?" demanded Walker.

"Talk to him," smiled Gerhart. "Buy him off if necessary."

Tom Walker snorted contemptuously. "I reckon I know Grizzly better 'n you an' the last thing anyone can do is buy him off with money. I've never known him have any and he doesn't seem to need any. He can live off the land and by beggin' occasionally better'n most men."

"He must have a price," said Gerhart, "all we have to do is find what that price is."

"And this stranger?" demanded Walker. "I'd say there was no way on earth that he could be bought off."

"Then we'll just have to think of

something else," said Gerhart.

"Like killin' him?"

Hans Gerhart pursed his lips, placed his fingertips together and slowly nodded. "If need be," he said quietly. "I don't want to do it any more than you do but if we can't persuade Grizzly not to say anything then we just might have to kill them both."

"You're mad!" hissed Walker. "You kill either or both of them and even if you get away with it, you'll have the law askin' all sorts of questions."

Gerhart simply smiled. "My friend," he said, "the difference between us is that I do not mind how many questions they ask. Questions never killed anyone and with Grizzly out of the way their only witness is gone."

Tom Walker scowled for a few moments. "I don't care, I don't like it. Robbin' the bank was one thing, even havin' Clay McKinley blamed for it was one thing and I must admit a brilliant idea, but killin', that's somethin' else altogether different. You can count me out, I want nothin' to do with it."

Hans Gerhart laughed scornfully. "My dear friend," he sneered, "you are already part of it, you have been ever since the clerk was killed."

"I didn't do that," huffed Walker. "That was your idea, you were the one who stood over him and pulled the trigger. Yeh, thinkin' about it, I think you even enjoyed doin' it."

Gerhart's laughter suddenly changed to a threatening snarl. "Just as I shall enjoy shooting you if you do not co-operate, my friend. Be warned, I do not make idle threats. I shall not allow any qualms you may have stand in the way of my safety and freedom."

★ ★ ★

Clay McKinley was surprised to discover Hans Gerhart's ranch house deserted but in a way it suited his purpose since he was able to make a search just in case there was anything which might point to Gerhart's guilt, although he would have been more than surprised if there had been. He made no secret of the fact that he had been searching and even less secret of the fact that he had opened a bottle of expensive Scotch whisky and helped himself to a liberal quantity. Then, with the warm glow of malt whisky inside him, he settled in a comfortable armchair with a commanding view of the road leading up to the ranch and waited . . .

★ ★ ★

Victor Smith hardly needed anyone to tell him where Grizzly Evans was likely to be found. He had seen the old man around town on more than one occasion and had heard stories about how Grizzly had been around since before the white man had even discovered America. He knew that the old silver mine was the most likely place he would be found since it was one of the few places that offered shelter and water.

"Good day to you, Mr Evans," called Smith as he lolled in his saddle overlooking a hollow where a bedraggled figure sat huddled over a low fire.

Grizzly Evans looked up sharply: he knew from experience that if anyone ever called him Mr Evans they meant trouble. "It was a good day," countered the old man as he straightened himself. "I ain't too sure 'bout that now."

"Most unfriendly," laughed Smith as he eased his horse down the slope into the hollow where he proceeded to circle the old man. He wrinkled his nose and spat on to the ground. "God, but you stink! Vermin like you shouldn't be allowed to roam loose."

"Nobody asked you to come here," said Grizzly. "If you don't like my company or the way I smell you can allus leave."

"I wish I could," sighed Smith swinging his leg across his saddle and sliding off, rifle in hand. "The thing is I've been sent to find out where you are."

"So now you've found me," snarled Grizzly. "Good day to you."

"That's only part of it," grunted Smith. "My boss seems very interested in someone you might know. I ain't all that sure why he should be, that's none of my business. There's been this stranger in town an' he seems to be causin' a few folk a lot of problems, not physical problems you understand, more a matter of just gettin' under their skin. I want to know who he is."

"How the hell should I know?" said Grizzly.

"Because I think this mysterious stranger has been sleeping up here," Smith said as he kicked at a bedroll. "Now I'd say you wasn't the type to use a roll like this, that heap of brush over there looks more like your style. Who is he?"

"One sure way of findin' out is to ask him," said Grizzly.

Smith laughed. "Oh, I think they've

tried that but he won't say. That's why I've come to ask you. I'm sure you two must have been talking."

"He didn't tell me nothin'."

Smith grinned. "At least we've established that he was here. I hope you don't mind if I don't believe you, Mr Evans."

"Believe what you want," hissed Grizzly. "I can't stop you."

"Indeed you can't," nodded Smith. "I must admit that I am not totally convinced that the only reason I was sent out here was to see if you knew who the stranger was. I think there's more to it and that you have a good idea what it is. I also think that it's something concerning my boss, Tom Walker, and Hans Gerhart. They both seemed very anxious that I found out where you were. Now I'm a man who likes to know what's happening, I find it useful sometimes when dealing with people. Why should they be interested in you? Why should a filthy old man like you get them worried?"

"Try askin' 'em," Grizzly hissed.

Smith laughed. "That would get me nowhere and might even end up losin' me my job. It ain't much of a job tryin' to persuade folk to pay their debts. Most manage to pay up somehow when I ask 'em, it's only occasionally that I get the pleasure of actually *persuading* someone. It pleases me but they find it very painful."

"Don't tell me your problems," said Grizzly.

"Oh, it's not a problem," grinned Smith. "Now, I suggest that you tell me everythin' you know. I want to know all about this stranger and, more importantly, I want to know why Walker and Gerhart should be worried about you."

"Go to hell!" said Grizzly, defiantly.

"It is more than likely that I shall eventually," laughed Smith. The butt of his rifle swung into the old man's face . . .

★ ★ ★

170

Clay woke with a start: he had not intended to fall asleep, it just happened and he put it down to having too much whisky. A wagon drew up outside and two figures alighted, one simply jumping off and the other huge frame having to be helped to the ground. Even accounting for her greatly increased size, Clay recognised Gwendoline Gerhart. Hans Gerhart had seen Clay's horse and approached the house warily whilst Gwendoline disappeared round the back, apparently oblivious to anything wrong. Clay remained in the chair although this time his gun was in his hand.

"Good afternoon, Mr Gerhart," greeted Clay as the door opened. Although Gerhart had been wary, he seemed totally unprepared. "I thought it was about time I paid you a visit."

"You!" exclaimed Gerhart. "What the hell do you want?"

"Justice," grinned Clay.

"Justice?" grated Gerhart. "If it's justice you want you should see the sheriff or a lawyer."

"It's too late for that," smiled Clay.

Gerhart casually walked across to a desk but Clay was quickly up on his feet and prodding his gun into Gerhart's side. He eased open the drawer which Gerhart had his hand on and took out the small Chamberlain revolver and slipped it into his pocket for safety.

"Nice try Hans," smiled Clay. "Maybe you should stick to robbin' banks and killin' bank clerks."

Gerhart looked alarmed. "What the hell are you talking about? Just who are you and what do you want?"

Clay prodded his gun harder into Gerhart's side and indicated the chair. "Sit down, Hans and I'll tell you all about it."

Hans Gerhart did as he was told and sat in the deep, leather chair staring up at the intruder, his mouth slightly agape. "Tom was right," he said eventually, "there is something familiar about you. The story is that you are Clay McKinley's brother."

"Does that bother you?" asked Clay.

"Why should it bother me?" said Gerhart, his mouth quivering slightly as he spoke. "What is it you want with me?"

"An admission," grinned Clay. "An admission that it was you, Tom Walker and Jim Proud who carried out that robbery and that Pete Turnbull was also involved."

Gerhart laughed nervously. "How can I admit to something that did not happen and that I know nothing about?"

"Then who did?" sneered Clay.

Gerhart shrugged. "How should I know? Clayton McKinley was convicted by a fair trial and jury. If you knew him you ought to know that."

"Oh, I can't fault either the trial or the jury," said Clay. "The jury had no option but to convict on the evidence. The only thing wrong with it all is that it was all lies, well-planned lies but all lies."

"And how can you be so certain?" said Gerhart.

Clay straightened up and stroked his beard, smiling almost tantalisingly. "Everybody keeps sayin' that they ought to know me, that I look familiar, even you. Clayton McKinley's dead, that's official, everybody knows he was drowned . . . "

"I did hear that the body was never found," interrupted Gerhart.

Clay smiled sardonically. "Bodies of men who ain't dead don't usually get found."

"Not . . . not dead!" Gerhart stared at the face before him, at first entranced and then slowly assuming a look of pure horror. "No . . . no, it is impossible. Clayton McKinley is dead, it's official, even the governor says so."

"Not dead!" intoned Clay. "Very much alive and standing right in front of you."

Hans Gerhart gulped and raised

himself slightly in his chair, a scream forming in his mouth but refusing to break forth; instead it died into a rasping gurgle as he fought the terror which was plain in his eyes. "No . . . you can't be."

"You'd better believe that I am or you'd better believe in ghosts," smiled Clay. "I think you must agree that I of all people ought to know if I robbed that bank or not."

"Yes . . . yes, of course," faltered Gerhart, "but please believe me when I tell you I wasn't involved with it. I can't speak for the others, but it was not me."

"I don't believe you," sneered Clay.

"Wha . . . what are you going to do to me?" croaked Gerhart.

"Kill you," smiled Clay, raising his gun to Gerhart's head. The man recoiled in horror and closed his eyes as if hoping that such an action would somehow protect him. "The thing is, they'll never know who did it. Officially I'm dead and dead men can't be convicted of anythin'."

"No, please, don't kill me!" pleaded Gerhart. "I . . . I'll make it up to you. I am a rich man. Think about it, you are dead and nobody need ever know otherwise. I'll give you a thousand dollars. Think of it, think of what you could do with a thousand dollars . . . "

"Piss it all away in no time!" spat Clay. "I don't want your money, the three years I did in prison is worth a whole lot more'n a miserly thousand dollars!"

"Two thousand!" countered Gerhart. Once again Clay spat on to the carpet. "Three . . . three thousand dollars . . . " Clay pulled back the hammer on his Colt and Gerhart squirmed and started to sweat. "Five . . . " he blurted out, "five thousand dollars . . . Please, take it, it's all the cash I have."

"Try ten thousand," grinned Clay.

"Ten . . . " gulped Gerhart.

"Yeh, ten thousand dollars," hissed

Clay. "That was the amount it took to convict me, the amount that was discovered in my house."

Hans Gerhart quite suddenly relaxed and even smiled. "OK," he said so casually that Clay should have known something was wrong. "Ten thousand dollars." He seemed to be looking past Clay but before he could turn something very heavy was smashed into the back of his head . . .

8

THEY met more-or-less midway between Gerhart's ranch and the town, Gerhart apparently very calm and composed but Tom Walker very agitated and sweating profusely. Whether his sweating was caused by the heat or his anxiety was a matter of debate.

"It's McKinley!" he blurted out breathlessly. "The stranger we've all been so het-up about, he's Clayton McKinley!"

"I know," smiled Gerhart. "How did you find out?"

"You . . . you know?" gasped Walker. "How . . . ?"

"He told me," said Gerhart calmly. "He came to my place."

Tom Walker seemed completely confused. "Wha . . . how . . . he came to your place?"

"That's what I said," smiled Gerhart. "I came home and there he was. He threatened to kill me."

"Maybe you'd better tell me what's goin' on," said Walker, gasping for breath. "If he came to kill you, how come you're out here now and where is he?"

Gerhart laughed. "He's safely locked up in my cellar. My Gwendoline can sure pack a mean blow with an iron bar."

Walker shook his head and sighed heavily. "Maybe I'm thick or somethin', but I don't understand."

Hans Gerhart slowly explained what had happened but even so it seemed to take some time for the facts to sink into Walker's confused brain. Eventually he appeared to assimilate everything and shook his head.

"So what do we do now?" he asked. "He can't just stay in your cellar and he probably needs a doctor."

"We kill him," replied Gerhart simply.

"Kill him!" exclaimed Walker. "Christ, we can't do that."

"We can because we have to," said Gerhart with a slight menacing tone in his voice. "Anyhow, how did you find out?"

"Grizzly Evans," gulped Walker, alarmed at the prospect of having to kill McKinley. "Vic found him out at the old silver mine and he managed to persuade him to tell him everythin' he knew. Not only does he know about McKinley but, like we thought, it was him who saw us with the money."

Gerhart smiled with satisfaction as it had been he who had suggested Grizzly as the most likely witness. "Where is he now?" he asked.

"Still there," said Walker. "Vic tied him up and left him inside one of the shafts. He thought we would want to talk to him and didn't want him wanderin' off."

"At least Smith is not afraid to act," said Gerhart slouching in his saddle. He 'hummphed' and slowly shook his head. "Now we know it really is Clay McKinley it seems obvious and I wonder we didn't realize it before, 'ceptin' we all took it for granted that he was dead so we assumed it had to be someone else."

"OK, so now we know," said Walker. "The thing is, what do we do with Grizzly now?"

"Kill him too," replied Gerhart calmly and with a smile.

"Bloody hell!" moaned Walker. "We can't go around killin' everyone just because they might know somethin' or say somethin'. I said when we robbed the bank that I wanted no part in any killin's but you had to go an' shoot that clerk. Robbin' the bank is one thing but I don't fancy swingin' on the end of a rope for murder."

Gerhart laughed sneeringly. "As I see it we don't have that much choice. If we don't kill 'em, we could both find ourselves doin' more years in prison than we have left to live. I for one intend stayin' a free man."

Tom Walker groaned and stared hard at the ground for some time before speaking. "Hell, what a mess," he almost whispered. "I think you're wrong, Hans. There was no proof at the time that we were involved an' there's no real proof now. It's McKinley's word against ours."

"What about Grizzly?" asked Gerhart.

Walker shook his head and slowly looked at the rancher. "It was over three years ago," he said. "The judge will want to know just why Grizzly never said anythin' in all that time an' besides, it's well known that he ain't exactly all there. I say we sit tight, let McKinley an' Grizzly go an' see what happens. McKinley was convicted an' he's an escaped prisoner. Fine, he's in your cellar, all you've got to do is hand him over to the marshal or the sheriff and claim you were just doin' your public duty. Yeh," he sat up straight and smiled weakly. "That's what we'll do. If he's handed over it'll all be in your favour. He attacked you,

Gwendoline hit him with an iron bar an' you handed him over. That'd all go to prove that we had nothin' to do with the robbery an' that McKinley is just out to blame us."

Gerhart smiled sardonically. "A nice idea," he said, "but I don't like it. I like things to be cut and dried, I don't even want anyone lookin' into the past. No, they both have to die. Look at it this way: there's only three people who know who the stranger is, me, you an' Smith. Nobody is going to bother looking for him if he disappears. As for Grizzly: how old is he? Nobody knows, all anyone knows is that he's been in these parts forever." He laughed. "Some say he was here before the Bible was written. So, he's an old man and one of these days he's going to go the way of all old men, except that he is more likely to end his days out on the plains somewhere and all anyone will ever find of him, if they find anythin' at all, is a pile of bleached bones. All we will be doing is helping that process along."

Tom Walker groaned and once again shook his head. "I still don't like it. Besides, what about your Gwendoline, she was the one who hit McKinley, what's she goin' to say?"

Gerhart laughed. "No need to worry about her," he said. "She knows exactly what happened, she always has done. She knows I was in that robbery and she's pretty certain that you were too. What about Cissy?"

"She don't know nothin', leastways not as far as I know," said Walker. "She's never even hinted at it."

Again Gerhart laughed. "Then I can guarantee that she knows," he said. "Sissy an' Gwendoline have been good friends for a long time, you can bet your life they've talked about it. No, I'm sorry my friend, there is no other way, we have to kill McKinley, Grizzly Evans and Smith."

Tom Walker's eyes opened wide and a look of pure horror came to his face. "Smith!" he exclaimed. "Bloody hell,

Hans, have you gone completely mad? What the hell has Vic Smith got to do with it?"

Hans Gerhart smiled knowingly. "Think about it," he said. "Smith is the only other man who knows McKinley. He is the only man who knows about us and the robbery, apart from Grizzly. He was acting on your orders to question Grizzly and he is the one who tied him up in the mine shaft. He is an intelligent man and it will not take him long to work things out."

"He won't do nothin'," protested Walker. "Anyhow, we can buy him off with a couple of thousand dollars. Besides, I don't think he would like the law lookin' too closely into his past."

"I'm sure he wouldn't," smiled Gerhart, "but I am not prepared to take the chance. Even if we do give him money to keep quiet, how long will it last? How long will it be before he's back demanding more?"

"He wouldn't do that," said Walker,

now not quite so sure.

"He won't have the chance," laughed Gerhart. "Tonight I shall take McKinley and Grizzly out to Saddle-Back Ridge and bury them. Nobody ever goes out there so they'll never be found. You can bring Vic Smith with you, tell him he can do what he likes to Clay McKinley, that should please him. We'll dig a hole deep enough to take three bodies, kill Smith and drop him in."

Tom Walker suddenly reined his horse round and dug his heels sharply into its side. "I still think you're bloody mad!" he called back as he galloped away. Hans Gerhart made no attempt to follow but he seemed deep in thought as he watched the hotelier disappear.

★ ★ ★

"You're back quicker'n I expected," declared Sheriff Joe Turner as Marshal Giles Wilson entered his office ahead of another, important looking man. "I thought it was two days' ride."

"Two days there and two days back," confirmed the marshal. "I sent a wire and the governor agreed to meet me half-way. Is he still around, the stranger?"

"We saw him this mornin'," replied Joe Turner, "but as far as I know he hasn't been seen around since. He acknowledged the other man as he came into the office. "Good evenin', Governor," he greeted. "I just wish somebody would tell me what this is all about. It's probably federal business rather than town business, but it would be nice to know what is happenin' in my own town. It seems to me this stranger couldn't've caused more of a stir if he'd been Clayton McKinley himself."

"Which is precisely who he is," said Wilson.

Joe Turner stared at the two men for a moment and then slowly shook his head. "You ain't jokin' either, are you?"

Giles Wilson also shook his head. "No, it's no joke. I recognised him the instant he crossed the street. Once, a good few years ago, me and Clay were out chasin' some outlaws an' neither of us shaved for over a week. I'm probably the only man who's seen Clayton McKinley with a beard. This beard may have been longer but there was no mistakin' Clay. I almost arrested him there an' then but somethin' stopped me. The governor's of the same mind as me, he doesn't believe that Clay had anythin' to do with that robbery. Even so, I thought I'd better let the governor know what was happenin' but I didn't send a wire explainin' as that'd been one sure way of makin' certain that everybody in the territory knew all about it. So what's happenin' now?"

The sheriff told them all he knew and the general consensus was that things had happened much as expected. The next question was what they were to do next as it was agreed that they could not allow Clayton McKinley to remain at large for much longer. A timid little man quietly knocking the door solved their problem.

"I beg your pardon, Sheriff," said the man, quietly. "I can come back later if you're too busy." He must have recognised the governor as his eyes widened in awe. "I . . . I'll come back, I can see you have a very important visitor." He was about to disappear when Joe Turner called him back.

"What is it Walter?" he grinned. "If you have a problem I'm sure the governor won't mind hearin' it too."

Walter turned, this time hat being fingered nervously in his hand, smiled weakly at the governor and nodded slightly. "Yes, sirs . . . I mean . . . well, it isn't really a problem, leastwise not a personal problem, nothin' that concerns me directly you understand, more somethin' I think you ought to know . . . "

"Yes, yes, Walter," sighed Giles Wilson impatiently. "But we do have some very important business. Get on with it."

'Don't be too hard on him," smiled the governor. "The sheriff is quite right, even a State Governor must have the time to listen to the common man sometimes." He slipped a reassuring arm around Walter's shoulders and guided him gently further into the room. "Now, Walter — I hope you don't mind if I call you Walter." Walter shook his head as he gazed admiringly at the governor. It was to become a talking point in Walter's otherwise mundane life from that moment on — the governor had put his arm around his shoulder and called him by his given name. "Well, Walter," continued the governor, "you plainly have something on your mind so let's be hearing all about it."

Walter looked about proudly, relishing the moment of his new-found importance. "Like I say, sir," he said, "it don't really concern me, not direct like, but I was in the saloon — I go in most nights about this time an' have me a couple of drinks an' a natter with some old buddies — I don't stay late you understand, certainly no later'n eight, my Martha wouldn't allow that . . . " An impatient snort from Marshal Giles Wilson made him gulp and look a little guilty. "Well, sir, I got to talkin' to that Vic Smith, you know, the one who works for Mr Walker over at the hotel. Well he goes in the saloon regular like, says he prefers the drink an' the company . . . "

"Get to the point, Walter!" the marshal snorted.

"Well, Smith was already pretty drunk when I got talkin' to him an' — I ain't sure how or why — but the conversation got round to Grizzly Evans."

"Grizzly Evans?" queried the governor glancing at the others.

"I'll explain later," said Giles. "What about Grizzly?" he urged the little man.

"Yes, sir," said Walter. "Well, he

said somethin' about Grizzly not bein' around for much longer an' somethin' about him — Grizzly that is — knowin' who the stranger everybody is talkin' about really was and how the stranger wasn't goin' to be around for much longer either."

"Is that all?" asked the marshal.

"Yes, sir, that's all," replied Walter, "although he did say that for such an old man, Grizzly put up one hell of a fight."

"Would someone please explain just who this Grizzly Evans is and what he has to do with all this?" demanded the governor. Giles Wilson ignored him and questioned Walter again.

"Think hard, Walter," he urged, this time his manner more friendly. "Did he say anything else, anything at all? Did he hint at anyone else being involved or what he was going to do next?"

"No, sir," said Walter. "Oh, sure, there was a bit of small talk about the hot weather, the beer in the hotel an' how he preferred the beer in the saloon, oh, an' about how he was goin' to have him a good time with that new hostess they just had at the hotel."

"Nothing else?" urged Wilson. "Are you quite sure? It could be very important, Walter. Think hard."

If anything Walter looked slightly indignant. "There ain't nothin' else, nothin' at all. I may not be too good on my legs these days an' I have to do what Martha says, but my memory is still good. I don't forget things. Anyhow, he didn't have time to say anythin' else 'cos Mr Walker came in an' called him outside. I saw 'em both head back to the hotel."

Giles Wilson sighed and patted Walter on the arm. "OK, Walter, thanks for tellin' us, you've been a great help, you really have." He pulled a five-dollar bill from his pocket and pressed it into Walter's grasping hands. "Don't tell Martha or else she'll have every penny of it."

The marshal waited until Walter had left the office before explaining to the governor just who Grizzly Evans was, although he had to confess that he had no idea quite how the old man fitted into events.

"Right now I'd say it was more important that we find Grizzly," said Joe Turner. "It sounds to me as though we might be too late already."

"If he's in the area and not in town," said Wilson, "he usually hangs out at the old silver mine." He looked out of the window and up at the darkness. "I suppose we ought to get out there and see what we find."

"What about Smith?" asked the governor. "Shouldn't he be brought in for questioning?"

"He can wait," said Wilson, a little impatiently. "What's happened to Grizzly is the most important thing. Joe . . . " he turned to the sheriff, "Are you comin' with me?"

"Try an' stop me," replied the sheriff. "I'll get Sam to keep an eye on things here."

"We'll let you know what happens,"

the marshal said to the governor. "It'll take the best part of an hour to get to the mine in the dark and then we've got to find Grizzly and he could be anywhere. There's about six shafts to be searched, 'cos I'll guarantee that Smith tied him up even if he didn't kill him."

"I'm coming with you," declared the governor. Wilson and Turner did not disguise their surprise.

★ ★ ★

"It's important that you don't let on you know," said Tom Walker to Vic Smith as they rode out to the Gerhart ranch. "I think this thing has gone far enough but I've got to go along with it, for the moment at least. You could of course refuse to have anything to do with it, it certainly ain't no problem of yours."

"An' still get murdered!" muttered Smith. "No man threatens me an' gets away with it."

"What about McKinley and Grizzly Evans?" asked Walker.

Vic Smith remained silent for a time considering his position. "If he wants 'em dead, he kills 'em!" he finally declared. "The thing is where does that leave you? If they aren't silenced you could end up doin' time in prison."

This time it was Tom Walker who remained silent for some time. "Hell!" he finally muttered. "What a damned mess. A pox on both Gerhart and McKinley. It looks like I might be on a loser whatever I do. Stand by while Gerhart murders them both and possibly be sent to prison as an accomplice; help him to kill them and end up on a rope or make sure he doesn't kill them and be sent to prison for the robbery. What the hell would you do?"

"Hang fire an' see what he does," advised Smith. "If he kills 'em and he's found out, the law has to prove you were in it with him."

"And if he tries to kill you?"

Smith laughed and tapped the gun on his thigh. "No need to worry 'bout me on that score, I can look after myself. Personally I'd be more worried about what he intends to do with you."

"With me?" queried Walker.

"Sure," laughed Smith, "why not? It sounds like he don't intend for nothin' an' nobody to stand in his way an' I'd say that if that meant killin' you as well, that's just what he intends to do. I figure that he's got some sort of plan to make it look like a shoot out between you, me, Grizzly an' McKinley except that we all end up dead."

"He wouldn't do that," said Walker, plainly uncertain.

"Then trust him," sneered Smith, "I sure don't."

The lights of the Gerhart ranch came into view and ten minutes later they were in the welcoming warmth of the Gerhart living-room each clasping a glass of whisky but all of them under the stern, watchful eye of Gwendoline

Gerhart just in case either of them should dare to sit down and soil her clean furniture.

"He's still in the cellar," said Gerhart. "What about Grizzly?"

Vic Smith glanced at Gwendoline Gerhart, making it plain that he was not at all sure if she ought to be listening. "Still there as far as I know," he said.

Hans Gerhart smiled. "Don't worry about Gwendoline," he said. "She knows exactly what has happened in the past and what is about to happen now."

"She knows everythin'?" asked Smith.

"Everythin'," said Gerhart. "Now, it's gettin' late and we still have to get out to the mine, collect Grizzly an' then get out to Saddle-Back Ridge. I've made up some torches just in case we need them, but it would be better if we didn't have to use them, you can never be certain that there isn't someone nearby."

"Are you sure this is the right thing?"

asked Tom Walker obviously becoming very nervous at the prospect of what lay ahead, a fact which did not go unnoticed by the others. "I still think it would be better just to wait and see what McKinley does. He can't prove we ever had anythin' to do with that robbery and I'm sure that any half-good lawyer could tear Grizzly's testimony to shreds. There was no evidence at the time so why should things be different now?"

Gerhart sneered contemptuously. "The difference is that McKinley is here an' not rottin' in some damned prison. Don't think you're backing out of this, Tom, you're in it just as deep as I am and we both could end up in prison. You can be damned certain that if I go I'm takin' you with me. So we do things my way."

Tom Walker sighed as he toyed with the glass in his hand, the contents hardly touched, finally placing the glass on a nearby table before straightening himself and squaring his shoulders.

"I'm sorry, Hans," he said with a slight quaver, "but you can count me out, I don't want to be party to no murder."

Hans Gerhart laughed derisively, obviously not at all surprised at the turn of events. His hand slipped under his jacket and reappeared bearing a hand gun which he levelled unerringly at Tom Walker's stomach.

"They do say a bullet in the gut is a mighty painful way of dyin'," he almost gloated. "Now what was that you said? I don't think I quite caught it the first time."

Tom Walker was alarmed and licked his lips nervously, but his resolve seemed to harden. "I think you heard perfectly well," he said. "Go ahead, shoot. I think you intended to kill me anyhow, just like you said you intended to kill Vic . . . " Vic Smith had not moved at all, but now he was smiling thinly as he nodded. "It wasn't no joke, Vic," continued Walker. "Hans said he had to get rid of you too."

"I'm way ahead of you," smiled Smith, "me an' Mr Gerhart had a long talk earlier. He's right, it's you who is the danger. I'm sorry, Mr Walker, but five thousand dollars makes me see things kind of different."

"Five thou . . . !" exclaimed Tom Walker, looking in disbelief at both men. "You bastard, Smith!" he oathed.

"That too," agreed Smith. "My pa was suppose to be some travellin' salesman but my ma could never be certain. OK, Mr Gerhart, what do we do with him now?"

Hans Gerhart laughed and produced some strong twine from a drawer and threw it to Smith. "Tie his hands, make sure he can't escape. We'll take him along with us. It won't take much extra diggin' to make a hole deep enough for three."

Tom Walker turned to Gwendoline Gerhart almost appealingly. "Are you just goin' to stand by an' let him do this?"

"It's your own stupid fault," replied

Gwendoline. "Your trouble is, Tom Walker, you've got no backbone, never did have and never will have. I knew from the start what happened and I backed my man all the way, which is more than your Cissy would have done."

"Does she know?" he asked.

"Not so far as I know," smiled Gwendoline. "She never let on and I never got round to telling her, I thought it best if nothing was said. She's like you, she would've been unable to keep it to herself and would have panicked at the first sign of trouble."

"Enough!" commanded Vic Smith as he pulled Tom Walker's hands behind his back and firmly tied them together. Hans Gerhart simply smiled and announced that he would bring Clay McKinley from the cellar.

9

BOTH Giles Wilson and Joe Turner had been out to the old silver mine on many occasions, in all weather and all times of the day, both when the mine was a working concern and since, but even so their progress was slow. There was no moon at all and they had to make frequent stops to guide the governor across difficult parts of the trail. Eventually, however, they were slithering down into the base of the mine.

"Not much sign of life," muttered the marshal. "I wonder where Clay is?"

"Not here, that's for certain," assured Joe Turner. "There's no sign of a horse anywhere."

"What about this Grizzly Evans?" asked the governor. "Doesn't he have a horse or a mule?"

"He ain't never had either as far as I can remember," said Giles as he dismounted and led his horse to the vague outline of the old washing plant where he tied the animal. "He always said he never trusted either."

Joe Turner hitched his horse alongside the marshal's and the governor eventually fumbled his way alongside them. "If I remember right," said Turner to the marshal, "there's eight shafts, three by where we came in, two over there behind the washin' plant, one somewhere over there . . . " He nodded towards the far side of the complex. "And two about halfway up the cliff face over there . . . " He again nodded but this time over to his right. "Do you know to any more?"

"No," said Giles. "There used to be ten but two of 'em caved in a couple of years ago. Remember, we had to dig young Mark Briggs out of one?"

"So where do we start looking?" asked the governor, shivering slightly in the cold air. "I'd forgotten just how cold it can get out here at night."

"Too used to a warm office," laughed Giles, "you've gone soft."

Sheriff Joe Turner was not on quite such friendly terms with the governor and did not join in the banter. "I reckon we can forget the two up the cliff face, the old tracks up to 'em collapsed a long time ago and I can't see anyone either forcin' Grizzly to climb up there or even drag him up."

"I'll go along with that," agreed the marshal. "It's a good job I brought a couple of oil lamps with me. Joe, you take the three behind the washin' plant and I'll take the two where we came in."

"What about me?" asked the governor.

"Only got two lamps," laughed Wilson. "You can either come with me or wait here. Watch where you're puttin' your feet though, there's rattlers all over the place. They're pretty sluggish at night 'cos it's too cold, but they can still sink in some mean teeth if they gets trodden on."

The governor automatically raised each foot in turn as if avoiding the threat and even when the marshal laughed he was not entirely convinced that there was no danger. He elected to remain with the horses.

Both lamps were lit and the two lawmen went in opposite directions leaving the governor feeling most vulnerable both to nature and to possible intruders. He felt even more alone as each dim light suddenly disappeared shielded by the entrance of a shaft. There were vague shouts from both directions as each man called into the shaft and after a time both lights reappeared briefly, floating eerily in the blackness as the marshal and the sheriff made their way to the next shaft.

★ ★ ★

It was Joe Turner's lamp which suddenly reappeared to the accompaniment of a loud shout. Since Giles Wilson was apparently still inside a shaft, it was the governor who answered the call.

"Found something?" shouted the governor. "Giles hasn't come out yet."

"I've found Grizzly!" came the reply. "Stay there an' let the marshal know as soon as you see his lamp. I'm goin' back inside to make sure he's all right."

"Which shaft?" called the governor.

"Middle one," came the reply and suddenly the glow of the lamp had vanished.

What was actually only about a minute seemed to drag into many minutes as the governor waited for the lamp to appear.

Eventually it did and Giles was soon almost running back. "The middle shaft," said the governor.

"How the hell do I tell which is the middle one?" grunted Giles.

"That's what he said," said the governor. "It was over there."

"I'll find it," grunted the marshal.

"You wait here just in case we need you or a horse." He quickly disappeared into the darkness leaving only the disembodied light of the lamp bobbing up and down.

★ ★ ★

"Is he bad?" asked Giles when he met Joe Turner.

"He probably looks worse than he really is," replied the sheriff. "He's a tough old-timer. He's tied to one of the supports and says he might have been able to escape by just pullin' but he was scared he would bring the roof down on himself."

"Well let's get him out," said Giles as he drew a knife," you lead the way."

Joe Turner went ahead for about twenty feet when he turned up a side passage for about another twenty feet. They were greeted in what at first seemed a very sarcastic manner, but Giles knew Grizzly well enough to know that this was the way he tended to greet most people. After a few grunts and curses from both Grizzly and Giles Wilson, the old man was free and complaining bitterly that his wrists and ankles were 'Bloody sore' and that he was frozen through. The two lawmen smiled to themselves as they escorted a seemingly dissatisfied Grizzly Evans from his prison.

"Not before time!" grumbled the old man. "I could've died in there."

"From what I hear," said Giles Wilson, "that's probably what was goin' to happen. I think you've got some questions to answer, such as why should Vic Smith tie you up in there an' what do you know about the stranger in town?"

"What stranger?" laughed the old man. "He sure ain't no stranger to these parts. I reckon you must all be blind or sommat. That's Clay McKinley."

"We know," said Joe Turner.

"So what the hell you askin' me for?" sneered Grizzly.

"We want to know just what Clay has in mind," said Giles. "We know he's out to prove he didn't have nothin' to do with the bank robbery an' that Walker an' Gerhart did . . . "

"An' Jim Proud," interrupted Grizzly. "Don't you go forgettin' 'bout Jim Proud."

"How do you know?" asked Giles.

"I saw 'em," replied Grizzly in a matter-of-fact way. He suddenly grasped both men by their arms. "Quiet!" he whispered and appeared to be listening intently. "We got company!"

★ ★ ★

Clay McKinley made no attempt to prevent Vic Smith tying his arms behind his back before being bundled out of the cellar. However, he was plainly very surprised to see, in the dim light from the oil lamp on the back porch of the house, that he was not the only one.

"What the hell they got you tied up

for?" Clay asked Tom Walker. "Have you been demandin' more than they think you should have?"

"Naw!" sneered Smith. "We caught him cheatin' at cards."

"There ain't nothin' worse'n a cheat," laughed Clay.

"Joke while you can, Clay," said Hans Gerhart. "In an hour or two you will be able to laugh with the Devil."

"Him too?" asked Clay.

"Him too," confirmed Gerhart.

Clay attempted a shrug, which he found a little difficult. "So what's he done? I thought you and him were in this together from the start."

"We were," admitted Gerhart. "Unfortunately for Tom, he chose to develop principles at just the wrong moment."

"I guess that means he was against havin' me murdered."

"Murder is a strong word," said Gerhart. "I prefer to think of it as self-defence."

"I don't think the court or the judge

will look at it that way," said Clay. "I'd do yourself a favour and forget all about killin' me an' give yourself up. I dare say you could get off with no more 'n five years, 'specially if I put a word in for you."

"Five years is five years too many," grunted Gerhart. "Come on, your horse is saddled an' ready."

"How do you figure in this?" Clay asked Vic Smith. "You wasn't even in Lewis when the bank was robbed. I think you've got yourself mixed up in somethin' that could get out of hand and bein' party to murder is just the same as actual murder. What's in it for you?"

"I've got five thousand very good reasons," said Smith. "Now do like the man says an' get on your horse. It's just as easy to carry a dead body across the saddle as a live one an' is a lot less trouble."

"I hope you got your money in advance," laughed Clay as he was pushed towards his horse. "Even if you did, you might just end up dead alongside me an' Tom."

"And you could easily end up dead right now if you don't shut up!" hissed Gerhart.

Clay guessed that he had hit something of a sensitive spot but for the moment he decided to keep quiet since it was more than possible that Gerhart would carry out his threat. Smith helped both Clay and Tom Walker up on to their horses before he and Gerhart mounted theirs. Gerhart assured his wife that everything was going to be 'just fine' and that he would be back by sunrise at the latest, then he and Smith led the other two horses out of the yard and into the darkness, Smith leading Clay's horse.

During the ride, Clay kept up a regular conversation mainly, as it turned out, with himself. However, he did learn that Grizzly Evans was to join them and that he, Grizzly, was in the old silver mine.

In the almost total darkness, time

seemed to have little meaning and certainly had little relevance, at least as far as Clay was concerned. However, when it became obvious that his questioning and chatter were becoming very irritating to both Vic Smith and Hans Gerhart, Clay decided that enough was enough.

★ ★ ★

"Almost there!" announced Gerhart as they passed a large rock which was known locally as Eagle Rock due to some imagined likeness to that bird. "Vic, you go and fetch Grizzly," continued Gerhart. "You know where you put him."

Vic Smith grunted his agreement and once again silence fell upon the riders as they negotiated the rough terrain towards the mine. In the past Clay had brought in wanted men with their hands tied and he had never really appreciated just how difficult it was to ride a horse under those circumstances.

As they began the descent into the rough workings it was really brought home to him just how hard it was to remain on his horse. However, after a few curses and dangerous slithers, they had reached the workings.

"Do we get off?" asked Clay.

"You just stay right where you are," ordered Gerhart. "Grizzly is going to have to ride up behind you. Go fetch him, Vic."

Vic Smith had already dismounted and was making his way towards the shaft, at first hesitating, uncertain which shaft was which in the almost total blackness, but he eventually found his way.

★ ★ ★

"Time's almost up, old man," Smith called as he entered the shaft. There was silence and he hesitated. "You in there?" he called. "Grizzly, you ain't gone an' died on me have you?" This time there was a distant answering grunt and Smith breathed a little easier.

"Don't know why I should be bothered if you'd died or not, you're about to die anyhow."

Since he had no light, Smith was forced to fumble his way forward and, just as he thought he had reached the side passage, there was a movement to his right and something round and cold pressed into his neck. "One sound and you're dead," hissed a voice. Vic Smith was no hero and obediently remained silent as another pair of hands seized his and bound them roughly behind his back. "You were very wise to co-operate, Mr Smith," grunted Giles Wilson.

"Joe, have you got his gun?" There was a grunt from Joe Turner indicating that he had.

"It looks like you an' me got some talkin' to do," continued Giles Wilson. "We know you're not alone, who else is out there?"

Vic Smith was more than ready to be co-operative. "Hans Gerhart, Tom

Walker an' Clay McKinley," he said. "I don't know what's goin' on, all I'm doin' is obeyin' orders."

"Tom Walker?" queried Joe Turner.

Smith gulped slightly. "No . . . no, I been workin' for Gerhart, but I don't know what this is all about . . . "

"We'll discuss that later," grunted the marshal. "I think Grizzly might have other ideas. Now, you just be a good boy an' sit yourself down here for a while an' don't go makin' no sounds to warn anyone." He did not give Smith time to reply as he forced him to the floor. "OK, Joe," he said to the sheriff. "You lead out as if you was Grizzly, I'll be right behind you."

The two men fumbled their way forward out of the shaft and towards the waiting horses. Their approach was heard long before it was seen and when it was seen it was impossible to make out who was who until they were right on top of the group.

"I reckon this is about as far as you go," said the marshal. "Hans Gerhart,

Tom Walker an' you too, Clay, you're all under arrest!"

A single shot rang out and Joe Turner crashed to the ground. At the same time Hans Gerhart was forcing his horse forward. A second shot followed the fleeing horse but appeared to be wide of its target and a second later Gerhart was lost in the blackness. There was a shout from the far end of the workings, immediately followed by another shot, another shout and then two more shots. It was obvious that Gerhart had made good his escape as the sound of horse's hooves gradually died away A few moments later both Grizzly Evans and the governor appeared, the governor leading their horses.

"He got away," said the governor, stating the obvious. "I think I hit him though, in fact I'm sure I did."

"He won't get far," muttered Wilson as he examined Joe Turner. "Can't see much, Joe, but it looks like you took it in the shoulder, I guess you'll live."

"Feels like the whole bone is shattered," moaned Turner. "OK, Giles, I'll be OK, you see to Walker an' McKinley."

The marshal walked over to Tom Walker, gun at the ready and grunted with obvious surprise when he discovered that Walker's hands were tied.

"What the hell's goin' on?" he demanded, checking that Clay's hands were also tied. "Clay I can understand but you, Tom, what are you tied up for?"

Tom Walker, like Vic Smith, seemed more than anxious to be co-operative. "They . . . he . . . Hans was goin' to kill me," he gabbled.

"Kill you?" said Wilson. "Interestin', very interestin'. Now why should he want to do that?" Walker was about to launch himself into a detailed explanation when the marshal stopped him. "Don't bother just now," he said. "We'll have plenty of time back in town." He turned his attention back to Clay. "Hi there, Clay, long time no see. We heard you was dead."

"I am," laughed Clay. "You can't arrest a dead man."

"Interestin' point," conceded Wilson. "I ain't prepared to argue about it right now, that's for the lawyers."

"I guess so," agreed Clay. "Do me a favour, untie my hands, I think my fingers are about to drop off."

Almost without thinking, Giles Wilson took out his knife and sliced through the bonds and Clay rubbed his wrists appreciatively. "You'd better give me a hand with Smith," he said, "He's tied up in the shaft."

Suddenly Clay dug his heels sharply into the flanks of his horse and, giving a yell of encouragement, surged forward. The governor raised his gun but was amazed when Giles Wilson knocked his hand, deflecting the shot harmlessly into the ground.

"What the hell did you do that for?" demanded the governor. "He's escaped!" By that time Clay had become absorbed in the darkness, the only evidence of his existence being the gradually fading sound of hoof beats.

"I know what I'm doin'," hissed the marshal. "There ain't a man alive who knows this territory better'n Clay McKinley, he'll catch Hans Gerhart far quicker 'n we could."

"But he'll probably kill him," grated the governor. "Marshal, I am State Governor and as such you are answerable to me . . . "

"Clay won't kill nobody unless he's forced to," said the marshal. "You ought to know that better 'n anyone. I knew he was goin' to make a break for it the moment he could. Trust me. If things don't work out, you can have my resignation."

"I shall demand it!" huffed the governor. "What happened in the mine shaft?"

"I'll go get Smith," said Giles. "You keep an eye on Tom Walker, but I don't think he'll be no trouble. We've got a long night an' a long day ahead of us listenin' to Smith an' Walker an' then Gerhart when Clay brings him in."

"*If* he brings him in," came the slightly doubting reply.

10

CLAY McKINLEY probably did know the terrain better than most men but even he was not prepared to attempt to follow Hans Gerhart on a moonless night. His sole intention had been to escape from the law in order to complete the task he had set himself. The fact that he knew that Tom Walker, Vic Smith and Grizzly Evans would certainly tell all they knew was not enough. Nor was it enough to know that eventually Hans Gerhart would be brought to justice. His pride dictated that he had to be the man who brought him to justice.

After riding from the mine workings, Clay made his way to a small cave to rest for the night. In the morning he would look for tracks left by Gerhart, safe in the knowledge that Gerhart would not have had the time or the ability in the dark to eliminate them.

The cave was in fact no more than a mile from the mine and it was just possible that Giles Wilson would elect to follow even in the dark and that he too might know of the cave. If he did not, Grizzly Evans almost certainly did; Grizzly Evans knew almost every stone and clump of grass for many miles around. He spent the first half-hour listening intently for any sign of anyone following. Eventually he was satisfied they had not.

★ ★ ★

The first light of dawn found Clay studying the slopes of the mine workings and, after some time during which he eliminated first one set of tracks and then another, he found what he was looking for.

At first the trail was plain, easy to follow although rather erratic in its direction which Clay did not find very surprising considering how dark it had been. However, he was slightly surprised when the tracks did not end in the obvious sign of Gerhart having rested up for the night. After about two hours of fairly slow progress, it became increasingly more difficult to detect signs and for sometimes considerable distances he found no evidence at all and wondered if this was due to Gerhart's ingenuity or the fact that out on the arid, wind-blown plain, tracks were very quickly covered over by the ever-drifting sand and grit.

However, he had more or less established that Gerhart was heading east and this fact seemed confirmed when he first of all came across some recent horse droppings, now covered in flies and beetles which would soon remove all trace that such a thing had ever been there, and a short while later a small cactus which had recently been trampled on.

There did not seem to be any point in looking for other signs, there was only one place Gerhart was heading and that was Saddle-Back Ridge. Anyone heading east would have to cross the ridge or face a long detour. He did not rush, it appeared that Gerhart had ridden all night and he knew that neither he nor his horse could keep going much longer. Both would need rest and water and, if his memory was correct, there was only one watering place and that was a large pool at the base of the ridge. After that it was about another two-day ride to the next water.

Hans Gerhart would know this as well as anyone since the land Clay was now crossing was part of the Gerhart ranch, a remote and rarely used or visited part, but nevertheless still belonging to the rancher. It appeared that Gerhart had bought the land simply because it was so cheap and gave him a feeling of power even to own vast acres of worthless land.

★ ★ ★

Vic Smith was wise enough to know that apart from a possible charge of assault, which Grizzly Evans appeared to be very reluctant to press, there was little anyone could do and, since he had been paid his $5,000 in advance and he felt no sense of loyalty to anyone, he had nothing to lose by telling all he knew.

Grizzly Evans, as was normal, had had to be ordered and cajoled into saying anything and eventually it was only the promise that he would not be called to give evidence which persuaded him also to tell all he knew. During the questioning of the other two men, Tom Walker had kept up a sullen silence but when faced with what Smith and Grizzly had said, and the fact that Gerhart had apparently been prepared to kill him, he started to tell everything.

Eventually, at about two o'clock in the morning, Giles ordered that the men be locked up and suggested that they all get some sleep, an idea much welcomed by the governor.

"It looks like Clay is in the clear," the governor yawned. "I only hope he doesn't do anything stupid now."

"Like killin' Gerhart?" suggested the marshal. "Naw, I shouldn't think so. He probably feels like it but Clay was a lawman remember, he knows what's needed. Mind, I suppose he could shoot him and claim self-defence and in the absence of witnesses there ain't a lot you or I can do about it."

"What about Gerhart's wife?" asked the governor as he mounted the steps to his rooms above the assay office, which was where all important visitors were housed since the building was the property of the mayor.

"I don't see as there's much we can do about her, even if she did know all about it, we can't force a woman to give evidence against her husband. Anyhow, she knows what's happened, Sam Gates went and told her."

"And what's your next move?"

"At daybreak I'm headin' out to Saddle-Back Ridge," said the marshal.

"That's where Gerhart was headed an' if nothin' else I'll be able to pick up their trails."

"Need any help?" The governor asked the question more out of a sense of duty than any particular desire to go chasing wanted men across wind-blown scrub land. He was quite relieved when Giles smilingly refused the offer.

"Naw, this is somethin' I'd be better off doin' by myself," he said. "After all, it is part of my job an' I'd hate to have to explain things away if anythin' happened to you."

★ ★ ★

Saddle-Back Ridge loomed large, visible for many miles and although Clay was still about five miles away, he proceeded with more caution although he knew from experience that anyone scanning the terrain, even from the top of the ridge, would have very great difficulty in picking out a lone rider.

For another hour the ridge did not

appear to be any closer but, after crossing a dry riverbed, it suddenly seemed to be on top of him. He did manage to detect a few signs that Gerhart had passed that way and, ten minutes later, he dismounted, left his horse behind a large boulder and moved forward, cautiously, on foot.

The ground dipped suddenly and quite steeply and Clay found himself looking down upon a large, clear pool of water, almost completely surrounded by high walls of rock, leaving only a fairly small opening which was immediately opposite. He settled in the shade of a thorn bush and surveyed the scene.

At first there did not appear to be any sign of human life. There were a few birds but little else, then, there was a sudden movement close to the water's edge and Clay silently cursed himself for not having seen it before.

The horse which had obviously been there all the time suddenly became quite visible, as did the figure crouched beside the pool. The figure stood up and even from the 200 yards distance that he was, there was no mistaking Hans Gerhart. It appeared that Gerhart was making preparations to leave.

Clay knew that he had to act fast. Once Gerhart was the other side of Saddle-Back Ridge, it would be all too easy for him to elude anyone following as the land which had until this point been fairly flat, broke up into a mass of gulleys, dried river beds and deep holes.

Clay remounted his horse and rode at some speed down to the pool, making no attempt to hide himself. Gerhart's reaction was much as Clay had expected. It was not until the first shot from Gerhart raised dust close by that Clay made the awful discovery that, in his haste to follow Gerhart, he had come without a gun of any kind. Thirty yards from his objective and after a second shot seemed a little too close for comfort, Clay leapt off his horse and threw himself behind a large rock. By pure chance, he realized that the position he now found himself in meant that Gerhart was effectively boxed in since he would have to come past no matter which direction he intended going. The fact that Clay was unarmed was something Gerhart could not possibly know.

"Looks like you're trapped, Hans," Clay called out. "Come on out an' give yourself up. I promise you'll get a fair trial."

"Go shit!" barked Gerhart. "I should've known Wilson would let you go. If you want me, McKinley, you had better come and get me."

"I can wait," replied Clay, hoping that Gerhart would not suddenly take it into his head to make a run for it, although his memory of the man was that he had never been a man of rash decisions, but then he doubted if he had ever been in such a situation as this before.

Clay looked about, looking for ways to get close enough to Gerhart so that he could rush him and tackle him by hand, but the only way appeared to take him about fifty feet above where Gerhart now was and he could not visualise himself leaping on any man from that height.

"Seems you wasted your money on Vic Smith," said Clay. "If I know men like him he's got your money safe somewhere an' at this moment is blabbin' out everythin' he knows to the marshal."

"He don't know nothin' that'd stand in court," yelled Gerhart. "Just like Grizzly Evans, he don't know nothin' either."

"Maybe you should've thought about that before," laughed Clay. "They may know nothin', but you sure got panicked into doin' somethin' stupid."

"A pox on you, McKinley!" responded Gerhart. "Why the hell didn't you die in that accident?"

"Pure luck," Clay laughed again. "Anyhow, you must've known I'd be free sooner or later."

"I already had plans for that," called Gerhart.

Once again Clay laughed. "An' now they've all gone up in smoke, especially since Tom Walker is probably blabbin' his mouth off too."

There followed a series of unintelligible oaths and obvious profanities from Gerhart which appeared to call into question both Tom Walker's and Clay's parentage. Gerhart was plainly very agitated and was working himself up into even more of a fever pitch. This was something that Clay did not particularly want to happen since it increased the chances of Gerhart doing something rash.

"Calm down!" called Clay. "Think about how things are. Even if you get away from me, Marshal Wilson an' now the governor know what happened three years ago, Tom Walker is sure to have told 'em. Where does that leave you? Are you goin' to keep runnin' all the rest of your life? You're too old, Hans. Give yourself up while you've still got a chance. You'll probably only get five years, maybe ten, but at least you'll still be alive. This way you'll more 'n like end up dead."

Gerhart snorted his contempt. "Walker is sure to tell them that it was me who shot the bank clerk. That's a hanging offence. No thank you, McKinley, I think I'd rather take my chance on the run."

"Your wife, Gwendoline," said Clay, changing his tack. "Don't she come into this at all?"

There was a short silence before Gerhart replied, "She'll be OK; she has the ranch."

"Don't you think she'd rather have you — alive?"

"Hush your mouth, McKinley!" rasped Gerhart. "Why don't you just come on in and shoot me? Come on, I'm waiting."

"I reckon I can wait longer'n you," laughed Clay.

Suddenly rocks were crashing down all around Clay, one even hitting him quite hard on the shoulder. He dived for cover and peered upwards to see three figures silhouetted against the sun. Who they were was impossible to tell.

"Havin' a few problems are you, Mr Gerhart?" called one of the silhouettes. "It's OK, we've got him pinned down. Anyhow, he don't look like he's wearin' no gun."

"What the hell's goin' on?" called Gerhart.

"Just helpin' out," replied the silhouette. "Looks like you an' me both got bones to pick with this guy."

Clay suddenly realized just who one of the three men above him was: Jimmy Two-Trees, the Indian from whom Clay had taken his horse.

"You keep out of this, Two-Trees," called Clay. "I don't think you realize who I really am."

"A no-good horse thief, that's who you really are. If an Indian had done what you done he'd've been hanged as horse thief but 'cos you is white an' you stole from an Indian, that's OK. Well it ain't OK, mister. Anyhow, who the hell are you? Not that it bothers me."

"The name's McKinley, Clayton McKinley, one-time US marshal. You've probably heard of me."

There was a brief silence while Two-Trees considered this information. "So what? You ain't a marshal no more, you was sent to prison for robbin' the bank. You was supposed to be dead so I heard, but it seems you ain't but that's your hard luck, maybe you'll wish you were."

By this time Hans Gerhart had emerged from behind his rock and was standing nervously looking up at the three Indians. "Kill him!" he urged. "A man has a right to defend his property and if he stole your horse all you're doing is recovering what's rightfully yours."

"You kill him, Mr Gerhart," laughed Two-Trees as he clambered down the face of the cliff. "He ain't got no gun; he was bluffin' all the time."

The other two slid down the cliff face and all stood over Clay, each with a gun in their twitching hand, giving the impression that any one of them might go off at any moment through pure nervous reaction.

"Are you sure he hasn't?" called Gerhart.

"We made it down an' he didn't shoot," called Two-Trees, "I don't see no sign of a gun." He laughed at Clay and bent forward to prod him with the barrel of his gun. "Now for a man who used to be a marshal I'd say it was very strange and very foolish to go after a man and not have a gun. I guess it makes quite a difference. Back in Lewis you was believed just 'cos you is white. Now, suddenly it seems the colour of your skin don't mean nothin' no more. What does matter is you havin' no gun an' me havin' one. What you got to say for yourself, used-to-be Marshal?"

"I'd say you better not get involved in somethin' that don't concern you," said Clay as he slowly stood up and brushed the dust off himself and winced slightly as he moved the shoulder the rock had hit.

"But you've got my horse?" grinned Two-Trees. "Don't you think that makes it my business?"

Hans Gerhart appeared, pistol at the ready, glanced at the three Indians and then grinned at Clay. "For a few minutes there you had me really worried. I was just considering making a dash for it and risking being shot. It seems there would have been no danger. Two-Trees is right, what the hell is a man of your experience doing coming after a fugitive unarmed?"

Clay smiled weakly and felt his painful shoulder. "Let's just say that I didn't have time to collect a gun. It seemed rather more important to get away from the marshal at the time."

"I know what you mean," smiled Hans, now full of confidence. "It now seems that I hold your future in my hands instead of the other way round."

"Only future you're likely to have

239

is if you give yourself up," said Clay. "Killin' me won't make no difference to that."

"For once I agree with you," smiled Gerhart. "However, in that respect I am determined never to go to prison but killing you will give me a great deal of satisfaction. It is something I had intended to do in the event of you completing your sentence and returning to Lewis. An accident of course. For now it will give me great pleasure to see you die."

"What about me, Mr Gerhart?" asked Two-Trees. "I got me a grudge to settle too, he stole my horse, remember."

"Are you prepared to kill him?"

The Indian glanced nervously at his companions and licked his lips. "I ain't too sure 'bout that, Mr Gerhart. If an Indian kills a white man, no matter what the reason, there is only ever one penalty, the rope. My cousin, Billy Wild Eagle, he killed a drifter who tried to rape his woman an' he ended up on the rope."

"Then what do you want?" sneered Gerhart.

"He stole my horse," said Two-Trees. "There ain't nothin' I can do about that now but it'd sure give me a good feelin' to mess his face about a bit."

"Be my guest," invited Gerhart. "Just make sure he's still conscious when I come to shoot him."

The two companions of Jimmy Two-Trees looked even more nervous than he did and one touched his arm. He had no need to say anything, the fear in his eyes said it all. Once again Two-Trees nervously licked his lips and even more nervously cracked the bones in his knuckles.

"You sure about killin' him?" Two-Trees asked, a little hoarsely.

"That's what I said," grinned Gerhart. "I've got nothing to lose. If I give myself up, even if I don't end up on the end of a rope, I don't think I could stand a long prison sentence."

"An' if you do kill him you'll be hunted for murder," Two-Trees pointed out. "We're with you if you just wanna give him a good beatin', but we don't want nothin' to do with murder."

"Then get the hell out of it while you can," sneered Gerhart.

Two-Trees cracked the bones in his knuckles again and looked at his companions who both shook their heads. "I only ever hit a white man once before an' I got me thirty days in jail for that even though the feller admitted he'd tried to cheat me. Didn't make no difference though, he was white an', no matter what, I got thirty days just 'cos I was Indian."

"And if you lay one finger on him I'll throw the key away!"

The voice boomed out above their heads and all three Indians looked upwards in horror. Hans Gerhart looked up and reacted in the same instant as he threw himself round the large rock.

Two shots rang out, the first from Gerhart's hand gun which, at that distance, was obviously ineffectual. The second was from Marshal Giles Wilson's rifle and raised dust close to where Gerhart lay.

"You don't stand no chance, Hans," boomed the marshal. "Give yourself up while you still can."

The Indians had automatically raised their hands and stared in terror at the figure some thirty or so feet above them. "Don't shoot, Mr Wilson," pleaded Two-Trees. "We ain't done nothin'."

"Maybe not," called the marshal. "We'll have to see about that. Are you all right, Clay?"

Clay did not have time to reply as another shot from Gerhart rang out, only this time it was not aimed at the marshal, but at Clay McKinley. How accurate the shot was was a matter of opinion. It certainly struck home as Clay slumped to the ground but it did not appear to have struck a vital organ. In the same instant the three Indians dived for the nearest cover and Hans Gerhart made a dash for his horse. He only managed half the thirty yard distance before another shot echoed around, this time fired by the marshal. Gerhart fell to the ground, made a feeble effort to rise and then collapsed.

★ ★ ★

"You'll live!" declared Doc Trimble as he added the finishing touches to his needlework on Clay's side. "You lost a bit of blood, not too much though, I've seen a lot worse survive. Mind, another two inches and your liver would've had a hole in it too and I'm not too sure if you'd've survived, not here anyhow, I don't have the the knowledge or the equipment for something like that. Pregnant women, kids with mumps and measles and broken bones I can deal with standing on my head. The occasional bullet like you just took ain't too bad, but anythin' internal and pulling teeth I'd rather not know. If you want teeth pulled, Stan Green, the veterinarian is your man."

"I ain't got no plans to have my teeth pulled just yet," grinned Clay, wincing slightly. "Thanks, Doc. What happened to Hans Gerhart?"

"I couldn't do a thing for him," sighed the doc. "Giles said he aimed for the head and that's what he hit. Mashed up Gerhart's brains a bit."

Clay grimaced slightly and nodded. Somehow he had expected to be pleased at hearing of the death of any one of the men who had set him up, but now, lying in bed with Doc Trimble putting the finishing touches to his handiwork, there was no pleasure, no elation. In fact there was even a little sadness, Revenge proved not to be sweet but rather bitter.

Actually, Clay had no idea where he was, it certainly was not a room he recognised and a moment later the question was answered when Kate Robinson came into the room carrying a bowl of hot water. She looked at Clay and smiled rather self-consciously and placed the bowl on the dresser.

"I see you're awake," she smiled. "Good, you can do the job yourself."

"What job?" asked Clay.

"Shaving that blasted beard off!" declared Kate. "I was going to do it and surprise you when you came to."

Clay stroked the untidy mass of hair around his face and smiled. "Yeh, I guess it's about time I started to look a little more human. Only thing is though, Doc's just told me I ain't got to use my hands and arms any more 'n I've got to for a few days . . . " He winked at Doc Trimble who smiled and nodded. "That means I can't shave myself, so it looks like you'll have to do it for me."

Kate blushed and tried to hide her embarrassment behind a towel which she had also brought in. "I'm not very good at things like that," she said. "In fact I've never shaved a man before."

"Nothin' to it," declared Clay. "Just

make sure the razor's sharp an' don't cut me too much."

Doc Trimble declared himself finished and promised to look in the following morning and smilingly took his leave of them both.

"Are you sure you can't do it yourself?" asked Kate, avoiding looking directly at Clay.

"Positive!" smiled Clay. "Now you just do like I say and everythin' will be fine . . . "

★ ★ ★

"At least you didn't actually cut my throat," said Clay as he examined himself in a mirror. He dabbed a couple of small cuts which still oozed blood. "I've done worse myself. Now, tell me, what the hell are you doin' takin' strangers into your house?"

"There wasn't anywhere else you could go," she said. That was not quite true, Mick Hartford had volunteered but the consensus had been that Clay was in need of nursing that only a woman could provide.

"Is that all? Well thanks anyhow," grinned Clay, teasing her slightly. "Now, what do you think of me without a beard?"

This time Kate smiled and tilted her head to one side. "I suppose it is a bit of an improvement . . . " She tilted her head the other way. "Yes, I can say that it is an improvement. I never did like beards anyway."

"Enough of an improvement to make you more interested in me?" asked Clay, taking her hand.

"Mr McKinley!" she said in mock horrors. "Are you making indecent proposals?"

Clay laughed. "Ain't nothin' indecent 'bout what I got in mind."

"And what, precisely, do you have in mind?" she said, blushing.

Clay released her hand and lay back, staring up at the ceiling. "Well, it's like this. For years I was too tied up in bein' a lawman to bother too much about women, especially takin' a wife, an' then I had me three years in prison which kind of put things back. Now, I reckon I'm in the clear an' I ain't gettin' no younger so I figured that it was about time I started thinkin' about gettin' wed . . . "

"And I just happened to be a convenient and apparently available female," she interrupted.

"Hell, no, that ain't it at all," sighed Clay. "I know there's at least three other women in this town who are ripe for . . . "

"I am not like an apple ready to be picked!" she snorted. "Now, I do have other things to do, Mr McKinley." She stormed out of the room leaving Clay wondering just what he had said to upset her. Eventually he shrugged and closed his eyes. He never did understand women and no doubt never would.

* * *

Three days later Clay was allowed to get up and to venture briefly outside. He had been told that a full pardon had been granted by the governor and that Tom Walker and Jim Proud — who had been arrested at his home in Boston — were to stand trial for the robbery and that both men had admitted their part in it. Clay was now officially a free man.

During the afternoon of that third day, Clay, who had been dozing in a wicker chair on the front porch, was suddenly and rudely awakened by the sound of a buckboard crunching to a halt and he idly opened his eyes to see the huge frame of Gwendoline Gerhart glaring at him.

"Afternoon, Mrs Gerhart," smiled Clay. "Hope you don't mind if I don't get up. Doc Trimble says I've got to take it easy for a day or two yet."

"At least you can get up!" she growled. "That's more 'n my Hans can, no thanks to you."

"Me?" queried Clay. "I didn't shoot

250

him, in fact I was unconscious at the time, Hans had just shot me."

"And more's the pity he didn't kill you," she snarled. "Everythin' was goin' fine until you showed up. Damn you Clayton McKinley, why didn't you have the decency to die in prison or somethin'?"

"Maybe he should've thought about things like that when he robbed the bank," said Clay.

"And maybe you should have thought about being killed when you came back here," she almost screamed.

Casually she reached down beside her and suddenly produced a rifle. Despite the discomfort, Clay sat upright and raised a hand. Coolly, not caring who was witness to her actions, Gwendoline Gerhart raised the rifle and took a slow, calculated aim. Around her various people were running, some calling out for the sheriff and others running simply to get out of the way.

"This won't solve nothin'!" cried Clay. "Think about it . . . "

"I've done nothin' else since Hans was killed," grated Gwendoline Gerhart. "Goodbye and good riddance, Clay . . ."

There was a single shot from somewhere behind Clay's head immediately followed by a scream of pain from Mrs Gerhart who dropped the rifle and stared at the blood soaking into her sleeve. Clay turned to see Kate Robinson standing behind him with a rifle tucked into her shoulder.

"Nice shootin'," said Clay with genuine admiration.

"I can do more than just make cakes and tea," said Kate, lowering the rifle and going forward to attend Mrs Gerhart. "My father made certain that all his children knew how to handle most types of guns." She examined the dazed Gwendoline and smiled. "Just a scratch," she said. "It looks worse than it is." Gwendoline Gerhart's response was anything but lady-like.

By that time both Sheriff Joe Turner and Marshal Giles Wilson had rushed up the street and demanded an explanation.

After some time and interruptions from well-meaning witnesses, they seemed satisfied.

"We could charge her with attempted murder," suggested Joe Turner to Clay.

"Naw," he said. "She's gone through enough. Just take her to Doc Trimble an' let him look at that wound."

Giles Wilson sighed and nodded and, when Mrs Gerhart had been led to the doctor's office he spoke to Clay.

"Clay, you've been a good friend in the past and as a good friend, can I ask you just one favour?"

"Anythin'," smiled Clay.

"Just get the hell out of this town," muttered Giles. "We've had more trouble in the time you've been here than we had in years."

"Thanks, friend," grinned Clay.

The marshal waved a dismissive hand and left. Kate stood behind Clay and rested her hand on his shoulder and allowed Clay to squeeze it.

"You know, for a man who used to uphold the law," she sighed, "You

253

appear to be curiously incapable of looking after yourself. How are you at making tea?"

"I can learn," Clay smiled up at her.

THE END

FIGHTING RAMROD
Charles N. Heckelmann

Most men would have cut their losses, but Frazer counted the bullets in his guns and said he'd soak the range in blood before he'd give up another inch of what was his.

LONE GUN
Eric Allen

Smoke Blackbird had been away too long. The Lequires had seized the Blackbird farm, forcing the Indians and settlers off, and no one seemed willing to fight! He had to fight alone.

THE THIRD RIDER
Barry Cord

Mel Rawlins wasn't going to let anything stand in his way. His father was murdered, his two brothers gone. Now Mel rode for vengeance.

ARIZONA DRIFTERS
W. C. Tuttle

When drifting Dutton and Lonnie Steelman decide to become partners they find that they have a common enemy in the formidable Thurston brothers.

TOMBSTONE
Matt Braun

Wells Fargo paid Luke Starbuck to outgun the silver-thieving stagecoach gang at Tombstone. Before long Luke can see the only thing bearing fruit in this eldorado will be the gallows tree.

HIGH BORDER RIDERS
Lee Floren

Buckshot McKee and Tortilla Joe cut the trail of a border tough who was running Mexican beef into Texas. They stopped the smuggler in his tracks.

BRETT RANDALL, GAMBLER
E. B. Mann

Larry Day had the choice of running away from the law or of assuming a dead man's place. No matter what he decided he was bound to end up dead.

THE GUNSHARP
William R. Cox

The Eggerleys weren't very smart. They trained their sights on Will Carney and Arizona's biggest blood bath began.

THE DEPUTY OF SAN RIANO
Lawrence A. Keating and
Al. P. Nelson

When a man fell dead from his horse, Ed Grant was spotted riding away from the scene. The deputy sheriff rode out after him and came up against everything from gunfire to dynamite.

FARGO: MASSACRE RIVER
John Benteen

The ambushers up ahead had now blocked the road. Fargo's convoy was a jumble, a perfect target for the insurgents' weapons!

SUNDANCE: DEATH IN THE LAVA
John Benteen

The Modoc's captured the wagon train and its cargo of gold. But now the halfbreed they called Sundance was going after it . . .

HARSH RECKONING
Phil Ketchum

Five years of keeping himself alive in a brutal prison had made Brand tough and careless about who he gunned down . . .

FARGO: PANAMA GOLD
John Benteen

With foreign money behind him, Buckner was going to destroy the Panama Canal before it could be completed. Fargo's job was to stop Buckner.

FARGO:
THE SHARPSHOOTERS
John Benteen

The Canfield clan, thirty strong were raising hell in Texas. Fargo was tough enough to hold his own against the whole clan.

PISTOL LAW
Paul Evan Lehman

Lance Jones came back to Mustang for just one thing — revenge! Revenge on the people who had him thrown in jail.

HELL RIDERS
Steve Mensing

Wade Walker's kid brother, Duane, was locked up in the Silver City jail facing a rope at dawn. Wade was a ruthless outlaw, but he was smart, and he had vowed to have his brother out of jail before morning!

DESERT OF THE DAMNED
Nelson Nye

The law was after him for the murder of a marshal — a murder he didn't commit. Breen was after him for revenge — and Breen wouldn't stop at anything . . . blackmail, a frameup . . . or murder.

DAY OF THE COMANCHEROS
Steven C. Lawrence

Their very name struck terror into men's hearts — the Comancheros, a savage army of cutthroats who swept across Texas, leaving behind a bloodstained trail of robbery and murder.

SUNDANCE: SILENT ENEMY
John Benteen

A lone crazed Cheyenne was on a personal war path. They needed to pit one man against one crazed Indian. That man was Sundance.

LASSITER
Jack Slade

Lassiter wasn't the kind of man to listen to reason. Cross him once and he'll hold a grudge for years to come — if he let you live that long.

LAST STAGE TO GOMORRAH
Barry Cord

Jeff Carter, tough ex-riverboat gambler, now had himself a horse ranch that kept him free from gunfights and card games. Until Sturvesant of Wells Fargo showed up.

McALLISTER ON THE COMANCHE CROSSING
Matt Chisholm

The Comanche, McAllister owes them a life — and the trail is soaked with the blood of the men who had tried to outrun them before.

QUICK-TRIGGER COUNTRY
Clem Colt

Turkey Red hooked up with Curly Bill Graham's outlaw crew. But wholesale murder was out of Turk's line, so when range war flared he bucked the whole border gang alone . . .

CAMPAIGNING
Jim Miller

Ambushed on the Santa Fe trail, Sean Callahan is saved by two Indian strangers. But there'll be more lead and arrows flying before the band join Kit Carson against the Comanches.

GUNSLINGER'S RANGE
Jackson Cole

Three escaped convicts are out for revenge. They won't rest until they put a bullet through the head of the dirty snake who locked them behind bars.

RUSTLER'S TRAIL
Lee Floren

Jim Carlin knew he would have to stand up and fight because he had staked his claim right in the middle of Big Ike Outland's best grass.

THE TRUTH ABOUT SNAKE RIDGE
Marshall Grover

The troubleshooters came to San Cristobal to help the needy. For Larry and Stretch the turmoil began with a brawl and then an ambush.

WOLF DOG RANGE
Lee Floren

Will Ardery would stop at nothing, unless something stopped him first — like a bullet from Pete Manly's gun.

DEVIL'S DINERO
Marshall Grover

Plagued by remorse, a rich old reprobate hired the Texas Trouble-shooters to deliver a fortune in greenbacks to each of his victims.

GUNS OF FURY
Ernest Haycox

Dane Starr, alias Dan Smith, wanted to close the door on his past and hang up his guns, but people wouldn't let him.

DONOVAN
Elmer Kelton

Donovan was supposed to be dead. Uncle Joe Vickers had fired off both barrels of a shotgun into the vicious outlaw's face as he was escaping from jail. Now Uncle Joe had been shot — in just the same way.

CODE OF THE GUN
Gordon D. Shirreffs

MacLean came riding home, with saddle tramp written all over him, but sewn in his shirt-lining was an Arizona Ranger's star.

GAMBLER'S GUN LUCK
Brett Austen

Gamblers seldom live long. Parker was a hell of a gambler. It was his life — or his death . . .